One Jar
of
Magic

Also by Corey Ann Haydu

Eventown

The Someday Suitcase

Rules for Stealing Stars

COREY ANN HAYDU

One Jar

of

Magic

KATHERINE TEGEN BOOKS
An Imprint of HarperCollins Publishers

Katherine Tegen Books is an imprint of HarperCollins Publishers.

Library of Congress Control Number: 2020948227
ISBN 978-0-06-268985-6

Typography by Laura Mock
21 22 23 24 PC/LSCH 10 9 8 7 6 5 4 3 2 1
❖
First Edition

*To everyone who thought they had to be someone
better, stronger, faster, more.
To everyone who helped them understand
they were enough, just as they were.*

One Jar

of

Magic

One

The best jar, I think, is the one filled with a thin layer of gray fuzz. It's the sort of thing that would get caught in the dryer, not caught in a mason jar, but I like how it looks alive, like it belongs in the sea attached to a rock or on the moon, nestled deep into one of its crevices. It looks like something you don't care about or wish wasn't around or has to be disposed of.

But actually, it's magic.

"What do you think it does?" I ask Lyle when we pull it from the closet. We were looking for one of Dad's scarves— the orange one that looks like someone made autumn into yarn and stitched it right up. Dad has an enormous collection of scarves, all of them hanging in different closets around the house, as if there's nothing else one might put in a closet. Our coats live on the living room couch and coffee table and TV stand, and our rain boots live on the porch and even our clothes only ever live in dressers and on top of the washing machine.

Closets are for scarves and jars.

I've drawn pictures of our living room, and no one believes that's how it really is. Maybe they think it's weird or ugly, but I've never lived anywhere without coats on bookcases and coffee tables, jackets hung on the backs of every chair, three or four at a time, our whole life in piles, right there for the taking. It's how my father has to live, so it's how we have to live. Sometimes I wish we could eat dinner at the dining room table or sit comfortably on the couch, to have a life that looked like Ginger's or even Maddy's. But then I wouldn't have my father. And the trade-off seems pretty fair. An extra-magical life for the low price of having to look at parkas and fleece jackets and down vests all over the living room.

The jar in my hands now is one I haven't seen before. There are a lot of jars in our cramped, messy home here in Belling Bright that have been hiding my whole life. When I find one, I want to know everything about it, like it's a family member I'm just learning exists, someone I might grow to love.

Lyle doesn't feel the same way. Not about this jar, but

not about any other jars either.

"Maybe it's to make things dirty?" Lyle says. He's turning the jar around and around in his hands, but it looks the same from every side. Lyle's a lot like Mom. He's been around magic his whole life, and he's captured a normal number of jars of the stuff, but he doesn't have a feel for it.

"Maybe it's for dreaming," I say. I feel like the spidery gray could look like the gray clouds that come in at night, that the hazy way it's floating in the jar is a lot like the way dreams are blurry and hard to explain.

"I don't know," Lyle says. "I guess you'd know better than me." He says it with a shrug, as if he doesn't care, but I think maybe he does, because the shrug is a little too long and his gaze meets the floor when he does it.

"Dad would know," I say. It goes without saying, though. Dad knows everything about magic. Or if he doesn't know everything, he knows more than anyone else, and maybe that's the same as knowing everything.

One thing Dad knows is that I am like him. I have whatever special thing he has; I am extra-magical the way he is. I think I know it too. Sometimes my toes tingle or my breath catches or my head rushes and I think, *Yes, there it is, my magic, my bit of something special. Just like Dad said I would have.*

"Show me the last jar that you captured," I say to Lyle. He doesn't have the something special that Dad and I have.

3

But he captures a few jars of magic every year, and he still has one left from last New Year's Day.

He lumbers back to the closet and pulls out a jar with a green shine to it. "I've been thinking of using it before we head to the lake this year," he says. "Not sure what it does. Turn something radioactive, maybe. Can magic do that?" I don't reply. I don't think he's really expecting an answer, and besides, the answer is that magic can do almost anything, if you capture the right bit of it and save it for the right moment. If you know how to use it. "No need to hang on to it when we're about to get a whole bunch more," Lyle goes on. He smiles at the way the green glows and how the strange sharpness of the light turns his hands green too.

"You really think we will?" I ask.

"I think *you* will," Lyle says. "You're Little Luck. You were built for this."

I wait for the tingling, catching, rushing. The promise of who I am meant to be. I think it's there. Maybe in the tips of my fingers.

"Well, that's what Dad says at least," I say, but inside, I'm smiling.

"Guess we better believe him," Lyle says, and maybe it was supposed to be funny, but the words drop and clunk and clatter. They sound heavy. Lately, everything Lyle says has more weight than it used to. I wish I could ask him why. But we don't ask each other why.

"Time to practice some more, Little Luck!" Dad calls from the top of the stairs, as if he's heard us talking about him and doesn't want too much more to come out of us. Then he's here, in the room with us, and he's taking up most of it, which he always does. It's what we love about him, the way he is always so *here*, when Mom is so often a little bit *not here*. She likes to talk about other places, other towns, even showing us pictures of places without magic. But Dad is here and now and always and urgent.

He has the striped scarf on today, and his oatmeal sweater, my favorite to borrow, and he's carrying his own jar of magic. He's barefoot. He is always barefoot.

Inside the jar there's a sticky blue magic, a texture and color I haven't seen before. "Is it for the weather?" I ask. "It looks like weathery magic."

"It looks—could it be some kind of friendship thing? Unity? It looks like it stretches. Isn't stretchy magic for bringing people together?" Lyle asks. He's trying. He doesn't want anyone to know, but he's been reading all about magic in his room in the early mornings and late at night. I know because he has a habit of reading out loud when he's on his own. He says it's easier for him than trying to read inside his own head. Because of that, my whole life I've always known what Lyle's reading. I listen through the walls. I don't even have to try very hard. We hear a lot, in this house of ours. Thin walls and loud voices and maybe the magic makes

5

sound travel; maybe it bounces off the jars.

Whatever the reason, I like knowing what Lyle's reading. Sometimes I think that knowing what someone is reading is almost exactly the same as knowing what they're thinking, or at least knowing what they care about. So when Lyle seems far away and annoyed with me and ready to up and leave and join some other family without a famous father and a sister who everyone's sure is going to be all kinds of special, I listen extra hard at the wall our bedrooms share, and it makes me feel close to him again.

"Can we show Mom?" I ask. Dad's not telling us what this jar of magic is for, and he doesn't seem to be gearing up to anytime soon.

"Be my guest," Dad says. "But she won't know."

He's right, of course. We show it to Mom and she holds it up to the light, the way Dad taught us all to do. "Dishwashing detergent?" she says. I think maybe it's a joke, so I start to laugh, but she doesn't laugh, so I stop.

"It's magic," I say, which she should know, which she *does* know, but sometimes Mom is so spacey I can't tell if she remembers even the simplest facts of our world: we live in a magic-filled town called Belling Bright. I am her daughter, Rose. I will capture magic for the first time in five days. It is starting to snow.

"Maybe it's dishwashing magic," Mom says, and Lyle's

the one laughing now, and for a second it's precarious, like it might make Mom cry. Mom is quick to cry. But she's quick to laugh too, and that's what she does this time. She laughs with Lyle and it lets me know I can laugh too, so I do, hard.

"Who in the world would need dishwashing magic?" I ask through my giggles.

"Someone who really hates washing dishes," Lyle says.

"It wouldn't be the worst kind of magic to have," Mom says, and I think she means it, I think she'd like to get her hands on some chore-doing magic. It exists, but it's mostly for beginners. Twelve-year-olds usually capture only the safest kinds of magic. The ability to get rid of bugbites. Magic for painting your nails without using nail polish. Magic to help you win your soccer game.

Some people never get any magic bigger than that, no matter how old they are. Some people only ever capture the simple and safe and silly magics. No one will ever tell us why. But we sort of know why, anyway. Dad says he knows why. He says you capture what you're meant for, what you're ready for, what you deserve.

We bring the jar back to Dad.

"We give up," I say.

"What is it?" Lyle asks.

"Can we take a night off from magic?" Mom asks. Mom can capture more than nail-painting magic, but not by much. She usually captures twenty jars of mild magic. And if Dad's right, then I guess that means Mom's meant for things that are gentle and easy. Sometimes she'll get a jar or two of something more—magic that can turn a blizzard into a flurry. Magic that can turn the flu into sniffles. Dad calls it de-escalating magic, which makes it sound especially boring and unimpressive. But it's respectable. And Mom doesn't seem to want more than that anyway.

Dad pretends not to hear her. Sometimes I wish Dad would be more like other people's fathers, thinking about things aside from magic and how to get it and what to do with it once you have it.

But then he wouldn't be Wendell Anders, and I wouldn't be Little Luck, and we wouldn't be surrounded by all this magic to begin with. Dad's famous here in Belling Bright—for his bare feet and his closets full of scarves and messy house and big booming voice and of course his way with magic. Other towns have magic, too. Most of the world captures magic on New Year's Day. But nowhere has as much as Belling Bright, and that's at least a little because of my dad.

Which means he's famous, and I'm a little bit famous too, for him thinking I'm someone special.

"Let's find out what we have here," Dad says. He twists the lid off the jar. It's a hard one to open, and he grunts.

When the magic comes out it breaks apart, the sticky blue hitting the air and disintegrating. I wait to see something. Or feel something.

And finally I hear something, but that something is Mom, and she's saying, "Oh, Wendell. Oh no."

"It's fine, Melissa," Dad says, but I have a feeling it isn't really. "It's for Rose's own good. She needs more practice."

Mom shakes her head. She looks at me and at Lyle with this *well, I can't save you now* look. "I should have remembered," she says. "I've seen it before. We've used it before. Back in college. Sticky and blue. UnTired magic."

"UnTired?" I ask.

"You won't need sleep," Mom says. "None of us will, I guess. Is that allowed, Wendell? Can you use UnTired right before the capturing?" It's funny, the name of the magic we just let out is UnTired, but Mom sounds downright exhausted.

"It's fine," Dad says. "It's to help us practice. Not cheating. Just more time to work on things before the big day." Mom tilts her head and scrunches her eyebrows. "We need as much time as we can get. Our Little Luck is gonna blow them all away. Capture more jars of magic than I did my first year, I'll bet you anything."

Lyle and I are quiet. We still don't know what the jar with the gray lint does. Or what the green light in Lyle's jar does. But we know what kind of magic we are swept up in right now—a strange sticky one that we didn't quite ask for and probably don't want. But when Dad's the one in charge, you don't say no.

You don't even really want to.

Two

There are places without magic. We don't know exactly how many, or at least they won't tell us exactly how many, but maybe it's a dozen or maybe it's a hundred or maybe it's even more because the world is very big and Belling Bright is very small and very few of us have gone much farther away than TooBlue Lake.

Mom's been farther. She's been to a place without magic. I ask her what it was like when we're both lying down in my bed, closing the book we've been reading together. We're UnTired but doing our bedtime ritual anyway. Mom reads books with me before bed just like she used to when I was too little to read on my own. We read a chapter at a time, passing the book back and forth. Dad's never able to sit still long enough to read in bed with us, and Lyle likes to read by himself, so this is the one thing that belongs to me and Mom alone.

"Places without magic are slow," she says. "Slow but intense. People look at you for a long time. They ask so many questions. They seem unfocused, too. It's hard to explain."

"And they seem sad?" I ask. I picture them as sad. Floating around, looking for something to do or care about. We think about magic all the time. We dream about it. It's what we do. It's the thing that decorates our home and it's how we dress ourselves and it's how we know what to feel about this person or another. It's a question we are always asking: *Is this because of magic? Is this color real, or did magic make it? What about this taste? Or the way the night sometimes feels so fast and sometimes lasts forever—might that be magic?*

"Not sad, no," Mom says. "Not exactly. Sleepy, maybe. They seem sleepier than us."

"They're tired?" my UnTired self asks. I'm trying to picture a town of sleepy people, wandering around in their pajamas, their eyes halfway closed, their voices mumbly with dreams.

"Good sleepy," Mom says. "Maybe not sleepy at all. It's hard to explain. It's different."

"Are you practicing up there, Rose?" Dad calls from downstairs. He knows the answer. You can hear everyone and everything in this house. He knows Mom and I are reading, and he doesn't love when we do anything he doesn't do. He likes when we are thinking about magic. "You know, I didn't open the jar so that you and your mother could find out what happens to some princess locked in a castle."

We don't read books about princesses in castles, but I know better than to say that to Dad. I don't say anything at all, and neither does Mom. She kisses the top of my head and stops herself from turning my light off.

I stretch my fingers. Sometimes my wrist aches before bed or when it's raining, and maybe it's going to rain tomorrow, because there's an ache now from the stretch. I look for the hundredth time through Dad's notebooks about what magic looks like when it's at the lake, before it's caught in a jar. I've memorized whole paragraphs of his scribbles. He's promised it will all make sense when I am standing on the shore in a few days, welcoming the new year by capturing my first jar of magic. Being the person he says I'm meant to be.

Hours into my studies, Lyle knocks on my door. It's late, but it doesn't matter when you are UnTired.

"Maybe she meant calm," Lyle says.

"Huh?" I had been lost in thought about jars of magic, hundreds of them lined up, and me, smiling proudly in front of them.

"Mom. She said people without magic were sleepy, but not tired. Maybe she meant calm. Or peaceful. Maybe—"

"You were listening through the wall," I say, but of course Lyle knows he was listening; he doesn't need me to tell him. I bet he always listens, the way I listen to him.

Lyle shrugs. "You're loud," he says.

"Okay," I say. We let each other lie sometimes. It's easier that way. "I bet they're scared in those other places," I go on. I'm thinking about last year when I had an allergic reaction to a nut I'd never had before. I'm thinking about how my throat started to close up and my eyes were watering and how I could feel my heart beating all over. For a moment, I forgot about magic. I just felt my body and the way it responded and the terror of not knowing what to do.

Dad was outside, as always, and I hit the window and he saw me there. He saw my hand on my throat, the color of my face changing from white to blue, and he grabbed one of the twenty teeny-tiny jars of magic he keeps tucked into special folds of his jackets and shirts and pants, little jar-sized pockets that Mom makes especially for him, and he held the jar to my mouth and told me to take a big breath, and he said *Let her breathe* to the magic, and in no time at all I could breathe and even the fear of it faded. By the time Mom got home, the whole thing felt a little like a memory and a little like a funny story and not at all like something to be scared of.

I still don't eat nuts. Magic doesn't last forever, and it's hard to know exactly when a certain bit of magic might run out. Some jars have magic that lasts a few minutes or hours; others have magic meant to last lifetimes. Generations. Dad usually gets long-lasting magic. That's part of what makes him so special. That, and how sure he is about what each jar might do.

In other families, someone might not know if the cloudy white magic or the silky silver magic was the right one for restoring breath. Or maybe they wouldn't have even caught magic strong enough to save me. In other towns, faraway ones without magic, there is no solution to the unexpected things that go wrong. Bad things happen, and then what?

"I'm scared sometimes," Lyle says. But we shouldn't feel any fear. If we're sick, magic cures us; if it rains when we want it to be sunny, magic dries us up; if we are hungry, magic bakes us a cake, roasts us a turkey.

"What do we have to be scared about?" I ask. Lyle purses his lips.

"Not scared," Lyle says. "But. You know." We aren't scared of Dad. But we worry about him sometimes. Which *is normal.* He's our dad. He's the most magical man in all of Belling Bright. It is a big responsibility. And that means we have a big responsibility, too. To make things easy for him, to make our home a happy place, to be good so that he has the time and space to focus on magic. He has the broadest smile and the boomingest laugh and the friendliest wave. He's the best person I know and probably the best person anyone in Belling Bright knows.

There's nothing to be afraid of, because as long as we are good and happy and easy, then Dad can be good and happy and easy too. The magic will be ours and we will be its, too, and we will be the magical Anders family and we will have jars in every window and in every closet and hidden in secret pockets in Dad's clothing, and it shouldn't be very hard to be good and happy and easy with all this magic everywhere.

Three

In our Global Studies textbook there's a photograph of one of the places Mom visited. There's a clock tower. It's brown. Maybe brick. The hands of the clock are long. Maybe bronze.

"How does it work?" Ginger asks. She's my best friend and she's good at asking questions that other people might feel silly asking. "Does it just stand there?"

"Just stand there?" Ms. Flynn asks.

"The clock. In a non-magical town. What does it . . . do?"

"It tells time," Ms. Flynn says. She has a smile on her face like she's answered this question before, and I guess maybe she has; maybe every year in Global Studies, she shows this very picture of a clock and waits for the first person to ask how it could possibly tick and tock in that non-magical town across the ocean.

"But with what?" Ginger asks.

"Inside there are wheels, and the wheels turn and make the hands go around and around, and sometimes it even chimes."

"Without magic?" It's me this time. A chime is a magical sound. Created by jars of magic filled with specks of gold and silver. We've all seen Chime and Bell magic. We've heard it every single day of our lives. Whoever gets jars of this particular magic is in charge of the clock that year, but it's been the same person, Greggor Barnum, every year that I've been alive. He's good at it. He loves clocks and he doesn't mind getting up in the mornings to make them ring out and wake the rest of us. People like Greggor Barnum prove that magic knows where to go, that it is finding us as much as we are finding it.

"These clocks work without magic," Ms. Flynn says. "They work with bells. With metal and the way it vibrates. Things made with human hands. A very precise art." She looks almost admiring, and it makes me nervous, but I don't know why. She keeps her gaze trained on that photo of a clock, as if somehow not-magic is something special. When everyone knows that *special* and *magical* are basically the same word. You can't have one without the other.

"*Magic* is a precise art," I say. "Capturing jars. Knowing what to do with them. It's all very precise."

"Yes, yes, of course it is."

"*Very* precise," I say. "That's why my father—"

"Why he needs so much peace and quiet," Ginger finishes for me. And she's right—that's exactly what I was going to say—but it sounds a little strained coming from her. Like she's heard it one too many times. And I guess we've heard it a lot, we've heard him say it a lot, but that's only because it's so important. Important things have to be said over and over and over again.

"If you want to be the most magical man in all of—" I say.

"Belling Bright is lucky to have him," Ms. Flynn interrupts. "You're lucky to have him. We're all of us lucky, to live surrounded by all these jars of magic. And a man like Wendell Anders to lead the way with them. But. Well. These towns without magic, these faraway places, they have their own—they—well, they make do. They have clocks that chime and the sun does come out from time to time, and sometimes, by strokes of luck in their very own non-magical kitchens, they make some delicious feasts." She shrugs. Ms. Flynn is like that. She likes to say something enormous as if it's no big deal. She keeps two jars of magic on her desk, fewer than the other teachers do. One has lake water inside that bubbles occasionally. One has a bright red light within.

We've asked her why she doesn't bring more jars. And she shrugs to that question too.

I don't think I've ever seen my dad shrug, and maybe that's why he's so magical. I decide I will stop shrugging immediately. I start right now. I still my shoulders and stare at Ms. Flynn and don't let myself even twitch or shudder or shift a little in my seat.

It is very nearly New Year's Eve, my birthday, which means it is very nearly New Year's Day, the capturing. Which means that I need to become the person I am meant to become.

"I'd like to visit a non-magical town," Ginger says.

"You would?" I ask. She's never mentioned wanting to go anywhere at all aside from TooBlue Lake.

"Sure," Ginger says. "I think maybe I'd like it."

"Me too," Maddy says. "I think I'd like it too." I should have been ready for Maddy to pipe in. She always does.

"Oh," I say. "That's—I guess—it could be interesting." I say it because Ginger and I agree about everything. We both like the color yellow and books about dogs going on adventures and looking at my father's jars of magic and guessing what each one does. We both think the same boy in class is cute and we both like to wear fuzzy sweaters and the fingerless gloves that Ginger's mother knits for us every year. So we need to have this in common too.

"I thought you only liked magical places," Maddy says

to me. I try to remember everything I've ever liked about Maddy. How good she is at painting nails and that she laughs at even my silliest jokes and that she isn't scared of anything, not even of being the new girl in Belling Bright or of capturing magic or of the scariest parts in scary movies. I list all those things in my head and remind myself to be nice. Maybe truly nice people don't have to remind themselves, but I do with Maddy, when she's acting this way.

"I don't know what I like," I say by accident. It's not what I mean, and it's not true, and I straighten my back and try again. "I mean. I like it here. And I don't know about out there. But my dad says if you have enough magic, you can make here into anywhere. So."

Then I shrug even though I promised myself I wouldn't. I want to be just like Ginger, and I want to be just like Dad, and I somehow want to be myself, too, but I'm not sure there's any room for me to be all three of us.

There's a long pause, and Ms. Flynn doesn't say anything to fill it up, and no one nods or agrees with me or says their father said the same thing, and even Ginger is just sort of pretending this whole conversation never even happened. I think I see her look at Maddy and smile. But maybe she's just holding back a sneeze or something.

Dad says that being special can be lonely. "No one understands you," he said very, very early this morning when we were practicing jumping and running in the front

Four

There is a firefly batting its wings against my palms, and Dad says that's how magic feels when you catch it. Like a flutter, a blur, a tickle, a whisper. I let it go after only a moment. It's not magic. It's a firefly. And it deserves to be free as much as anyone else.

I've been practicing for New Year's Day by chasing fireflies and catching them with my hands. I let them bat against my palms for a single moment, imagining that they are magic, and then I release them, knowing they aren't magic at all. *Just because something looks like magic or feels like magic doesn't make it magic*, Dad's always saying. *Don't be fooled. You don't get this many jars of magic by chasing something else entirely.* It's at that point that he always waves to the jars. Dozens and dozens of them lined up on our windowsills, on the mantel, on the high shelves of the bookcase.

Soon, I'll add five or ten, or maybe, like Dad did on his first year, twenty-three.

The thought gives me a rush.

I practice for New Year's Day barefoot, even when it's cold. I don't have gloves or a practice jar or a net or Ginger's high leaps or Lyle's ability to see magic where most people only see air. I don't have anything but the way Dad looks at me—like he's sure I'm something special. Like he's sure I'm his.

It's cold tonight, a few nights before we travel to the shore to capture jars of magic. It's so cold I have on three sweaters—one is mine, one is my mother's, and one is my father's. The top layer—my father's—is a thick beige cardigan that smells like him: bacon and sugar and the woods. It might be a lucky sweater. Anything of his might be lucky, so I've wrapped his gray plaid scarf around my neck three times and I'm wearing his wool hat, too. It's brown and threadbare and not keeping my ears very warm at all, but my father is the best capturer I know, the best capturer anyone knows, so it's worth doing everything I can to be just like him.

"Rose," Mom calls out from the kitchen window. "Shoes. Please."

"You know I can't," I say.

"You'll freeze."

"Dad's never frozen."

"That's true!" I hear Dad call. He's probably sitting at the kitchen table, polishing jars of magic, readying himself to capture another few dozen jars on New Year's Day. "Bare feet make all the difference. Let the girl practice however she wants. Her toes will be fine. Rose? Pack some socks in your pockets for an emergency to make your mother happy, okay?" I can hear his smile. It's just as easy to hear my father's smile as it is to see it, a fact about him that I love.

"Do you have some I could borrow?" I ask. "Lucky socks?"

"Gross!" Lyle calls out. He's not practicing. He's sitting in the window seat and watching me work. It's his third year capturing magic, and he's done fine every year without so much as thinking about footwork or smelling the air or how a firefly feels when it's asking your hands to let it go.

He's done fine, but Dad and I are meant for being more than fine.

"You don't need lucky socks," Dad says. "You're the luck." The year I was born was his best year ever. I came into the world only a few hours before New Year's Day, and he said he caught them for me. One hundred sixty-one jars of magic. We've used most of them, but a few special ones are in my closet, on Dad's dresser, tucked into cabinets next to canisters of sugar and pasta and oatmeal. Mom always jokes that she may someday accidentally bake a batch of cookies with magic instead of flour, but it would be a hard mistake to make. Jars of food are heavy and plain. Jars of magic are practically weightless and filled with things like beams of light and the smell of the ocean and dandelion seeds, the kind blown from the stem when making a wish. The kind that look like discarded bits of clouds.

"Our children are *both* the luck," Mom says, which is what she always says when Dad calls me Little Luck. She says it for Lyle's benefit, but I'm not sure Lyle cares. He shrugs now and turns the page of a heavy book. He scratches a place behind his ear. He hums some song that all the kids at school are into lately.

Dad comes outside. He takes off his shoes and digs his feet into the ground. "You've got this, Little Luck," he says. "Close your eyes. Try to hear the magic." Dad says magic sounds like someone blowing an eyelash off their finger. He says sometimes it sounds like a wind chime, if you shrunk the noise and turned it to air. I close my eyes and listen. When I hear nothing, I close them tighter, so tight my head beats and my feet lose their focus and my face scrunches up. "You hear that?" Dad says. I'd bet anything his eyes are closed too, but I'm not about to open mine and look. "The magic is close. The days are dwindling. It's almost time."

I hold my nose, because I've heard that some senses get stronger when others are stopped. I try to stop breathing altogether. I bow my head and imagine my ears to be bigger and bigger and bigger, big enough to hear the faraway magic gathering on the shores of TooBlue Lake.

But all I hear is Mom stirring a pot of soup on the stove and Lyle turning another page in his book and the beating of my own heart, so loud and fast it must be drowning out the delicate, sweet sound of magic.

"You hear it, right, Little Luck?" Dad asks.

"Yes," I say, the lie sort of sticky and sour in my mouth. "Loud and clear."

Five

*What I Am Thinking About When I Can't Sleep After Not
Hearing Magic Once Again*

When Lyle turned twelve, I was nine and no one was
practicing capturing magic on the front lawn or the back
lawn or anywhere near our house.

On New Year's Eve that year, we celebrated my birthday
like always, and Lyle sang extra loud when the cake came
out. I thought he'd be mad, that I was getting attention on
a night that should have belonged to him. He was about to
capture magic for the very first time, and I was just turning
nine, which isn't even a very exciting age to turn. It's not like
ten or twelve or thirteen or an age that actually matters.

But Lyle doesn't always do what I think he'll do. He looks a little like my dad, with big hands and long hair that goes into his eyes, so that can confuse me, and I expect him to act like my dad.

But Lyle isn't anything like my dad, and sometimes I think that's actually kind of lucky.

"Where are the candles?" Lyle asked when the cake was set down in front of me. "She needs to make a wish."

"Candles?" Dad said. He'd been the one in charge of the cake. Magicking it up and deciding how it should be decorated and I guess probably lighting the candles too. Dad loved our birthdays. He'd make up a special song every year, about me and all the things I loved to do. He always brought a special jar of magic back especially for me the next day, and he'd call it my birthday jar and let me keep it in my room. He took the cake seriously. It had to look as special as a birthday was.

He brought it out to the kitchen table this time. He had a big smile on his face because the cake looked completely spectacular. It was three layers and neon pink with glittery purple sugar all over it. Except the sugar wasn't just purple and glittery; it changed colors, traveling through the rainbow like it was showing off.

Magic cake.

"Candles, honey," Mom said. "Cakes need candles."

29

"A birthday's not a birthday without wishes," Lyle said. He looked especially disappointed, and I remembered that Dad had forgotten *his* birthday candles that year, too.

And maybe the year before, as well.

"We don't need wishes," Dad said. "We have magic."

"It's not about that," Lyle said. "It's just what you do. On birthdays. To make them special."

"It's okay," I said, because I was watching Dad's shoulders go from loose to tight, his face go from smiling to that other thing, and I didn't care about candles.

Not really.

Maybe only a little. I liked the way they flickered and how you always knew the smell, how birthday candles smelled and looked different than any other kind of candles. I liked picking out wishes, except I always wished for the same thing.

"I thought a magical cake would make things special, Lyle," Dad said. "I thought everything I do for this family made things special."

"I can get the candles," Mom said. She started walking toward the kitchen, but Dad blocked her.

"Is there more you need to say, Lyle?" Dad asked.

Lyle shook his head. Dad was under a lot of pressure, being in charge of all that magic, and sometimes he needed a minute to cool off and we needed to stop bothering him, and I don't know how Lyle forgot all of that that one day, but he did. Because the next thing he said was, "Can't you do any-thing the normal way? Can't you give us one normal thing? Candles on a cake? Like every other kid in the world gets?"

We never ate that cake. Not one crumb of it. After Lyle said what he said, Dad threw the whole thing in the trash. There's not really any way to fix a birthday, once the cake is in the trash.

Lyle and I stayed up late that night, even though he really should have gotten rest for his first New Year's Day capturing. We threw acorns at trees from this little patch of roof we could get to from my bedroom window.

"Why'd you do that?" I asked.

"I wanted you to be able to make your wish. You love wishing on birthday candles," Lyle said.

I nodded. It was a small thing that was actually very big.

"You shouldn't have—" I started, but Lyle knew I meant *thank you for seeing and knowing and protecting me.*

"He's stressed out," Lyle said.

"He hasn't slept much," I said.

"He'll be better after the capturing."

"It was just a cake."

"It was kind of funny."

"I don't even like pink," I said.

"Me neither," Lyle said, and that was it; we didn't have to say anything more.

We never have to say much, Lyle and I.

31

Six

"Can you help me find someone?"

The woman who says it is in jeans and brown shoes that look brand-new and expensive. Maybe she magicked them up this morning. Jars with dirt inside sometimes conjure up boots or growth or good health. I'm not sure what kind of magic would make her kind of shoe, what you'd have to whisper to make it fit just right, but I'm sure it exists. It all exists. No two jars are exactly the same; every bit of magic has its own use, and its own personality, too.

"Like people," Mom's always saying, but Dad never agrees.

"Magic isn't like people at all," he says. "Magic is only like magic. Nothing else like it in the whole world. No way to imitate it. No way to capture it except with your own two unmagical hands. No way to create it. The most beautiful thing in our world."

The conversation always stops there, but the last time they had it I almost asked why Dad thinks magic is so much better than people, why it would be an insult to think magic and people have anything in common at all.

But our job isn't to ask a million questions about why magic is the way it is. Our job is to find the magic, to let it find us, and to study hard to pin down what each jar can be used for. Our job is to trust the magic.

Sometimes it goes wrong, like when people ask for a meal of fish and vegetables and end up in an aquarium. Or try to magic up a good grade on a French test and end up in France. "Magic knows what we need," Dad's always saying, "but we're not always so good at listening to what it's telling us."

This woman with the maybe magical shoes has a notebook in one hand and an empty jar in the other and she seems decidedly out of place on the school playground, where shoes like that won't let her run or jump or play foursquare or go down the twisty slide.

My best friend, Ginger, knows the woman is talking to me, not her, and she lets out one *hmph* of a laugh, a sound that's stuck between thinking something's funny and thinking it's annoying. We've been blowing bubbles, which would

33

be a babyish thing to do if it didn't involve trying to catch the bubble in a mason jar without popping it. My dad swears by it as the best way to practice capturing magic. I'm especially good at catching the shiny suds in my UnTired state. Ginger is especially not-good at it. She drops jars. She runs into bubbles. She trips over her own feet when she's trying to move quickly.

But she can sure jump high, and she does, now. The woman and I watch her impossible leaps together. If we didn't know better, we'd be wondering if that was some kind of magic, too. But no one's allowed to use magic to get magic-capturing skills. Not for themselves. Not for their kids, either. That's why Mom was worried about the UnTired magic helping us too much. But if Dad said it's fine, it must be fine. Dad knows everything about magic and rules and takes it all very seriously. So I do too.

"Who are you looking for?" I ask the woman in the brown shoes. I want to pretend she could be looking for someone else entirely: a girl who is known for her basketball skills, or the new girl in town, or a girl who is about to hear terrible, tragic news from a stranger in the middle of the playground. But in reality it's me; it's only ever me.

"Rose Alice Anders," she says, pronouncing each part of my name with the precision of a tailor or a glassblower or my father once a year when he's capturing magic. "She's also known as Little Luck. I don't know if that's what you

34

kids call her. Do you know her?"

"It's *her*," Ginger says, laughing, loosening her shoulders and shaking her head and nudging me. "This is Rose. We don't call her Little Luck. Only her dad calls her that."

"Oh!" The woman adjusts the collar of her shirt and brushes her hands through her hair. "Well. Rose. Rose Alice. I've been wanting to talk to you for a long time."

There's only one reason a woman like this would want to talk to a girl like me, and Dad's been warning me about it for the last few weeks.

"They'll ask you questions. They'll want to know about me. About Mom. About Lyle, even. They'll want to know your tricks and your feelings and what you are afraid of and what you hope for. They'll make you guess how many jars you're going to capture. They'll ask if I'm hard on you, if you like being Little Luck, if you think you're special." Dad said it just like that, all in one enormous breath, and when he got to the end he looked at me extra hard to make sure I'd heard. I had. "Don't answer their questions. Don't let them in," he said to me over ice cream sundaes, and used his gentle voice. Sometimes Dad's advice felt like a hug—warm and safe. I wished he could be there every time something confusing or hard happened, but he always tried to help me be prepared for when he wasn't there.

I adjust the scarf of his that's around my neck now. His red one, which is sleepy-soft and rail-thin. I bet she'd like to know it's his. I wiggle my toes and try to guess how many jars of magic she caught last year. Not many. Maybe eleven or twelve. Probably nothing very powerful or interesting. Her shoes are too pointy and her hair is too straight and she's too nervous to be good at the things Dad and I are good at. She tells me again how long she's been waiting to talk to me.

"I've never really wanted to talk to you," I say. It comes out sort of mean. I know because Ginger stiffens and the lady frowns and my heart does a dip-dive-twist that it does when I know I've messed up. "I mean, I don't know you. But I don't like to talk to strangers. I'm not allowed." This is much better, and I watch Ginger and the lady both relax. They nod. I nod back.

"I'm a reporter," the lady says. "Do you know what that is?"

"I'm turning twelve tomorrow," I say. "*Twelve*." This is probably a little mean too. But I'm basically twelve, and I don't like the way her voice is singsongy and how she bends her knees when she talks to me, like she's making sure I know how tiny I am.

"Of course you are!" she says. "That's why I'm here. To see how you're feeling about New Year's Day. About your first year. About everything ahead for you."

I can't help but smile. Dad said to be careful around reporters, and my own smart heart says this woman isn't my friend, but I love thinking about New Year's Day and what's to come. I love imagining January 2 and January 3, when I will be lining up jars of magic in our windows and everyone will know they are mine. Then I'll finally be the person everyone's been waiting for me to be.

I am ready to be that person, instead of this person, who holds her arms a little funny at her sides and doesn't ever know the right thing to say and thinks her best friend might be wanting to have a new best friend.

"No comment," Ginger says, saving me from accidentally telling this lady some little bit about my hopes and dreams. Ginger knows better than anyone how to keep things like that locked up tight and far away from people in fancy shoes and silly voices.

The lady lingers, but we stay still, like we're playing a game of freeze tag that she doesn't know we're playing. Eventually it works and she seems so uncomfortable that she leaves us be.

"Little Luck," Ginger says. "When will they stop with all that?"

It's not quite the same question I have, but close enough, so I shrug.

"I bet she'll try to interview *you* next time," I say, even though we both know that's not true. I think Ginger's amazing, but she doesn't have a special nickname or a whole story built around the day she was born. She doesn't have a kind-of-famous dad. She doesn't have a dad at all, anymore. My heart always squeezes at that fact even though it's been almost a year.

"There's a reporter!" someone says, sprinting up to us, and that someone is Maddy, and she, as usual, doesn't know that we've already decided how we feel about things. She's never on the right page with us, and usually Ginger and I laugh about it a little behind her back, but today Ginger just changes the subject to what the prettiest kind of magic is.

We all agree that it's the kind of magic that you almost can't see aside from the way it glows. Like moonlight in a jar. Even Maddy, with her neon yellow shirt and fourteen sparkly bracelets and hair in a high-high-high ponytail knows that with magic, it's best to be a little hard to pin down, a little unknowable.

"I hope you didn't tell her anything, Maddy," I say.

"What do you mean?" Maddy asks.

"We don't talk to reporters," Ginger says.

"We don't?" Maddy says.

"Reporters always want to know about Rose," Ginger says.

"And she doesn't like anyone to know stuff about her?" Maddy asks. They're talking about me like I'm not right here. I wave, to remind them that I am. Maddy sees, and finally speaks to me directly. "I said we're friends. And that you are just like your dad and everyone knows it."

"That's . . . that's okay, right, Rose?" Ginger asks, but her face is worried and she knows it's really sort of not okay at all.

"I'm not *just* like my dad," I say. I was born with his blue eyes and brown curly hair and long lashes. We both have loud laughs and shoulders that don't know how to shrug and we like thick sweaters and long scarves and the way it feels to try for something but not let anyone know how hard you're trying.

Still, sometimes when people tell me I'm just like him my stomach turns. I told Ginger about the sort of sick feeling and she said it's probably nerves. But it's something else too, something I don't quite know how to put words to because the other thing my father and I have in common is that we aren't very good at remembering the words to explain the way we feel.

"I thought you'd like me saying that," Maddy says. "I thought you were like, obsessed with your dad. Everyone's obsessed with your dad. I figured it was a big compliment." Maddy gets this look on her face—a deep frown accompanied by big eyes. Ginger and I used to call it her Please Like Me Face, but the last time I tried to use that phrase with Ginger she got all funny, rolling her eyes like she wasn't the one who made it up in the first place, like she hadn't said it a hundred times before.

"It's a lot of pressure," Ginger says, talking to Maddy in

the same nice voice she uses with me when I'm feeling sad or scared or mad about something that I can't quite put my finger on. "Rose's dad gets mad if we say too much. And we don't like to get Rose's dad mad."

All of a sudden I feel flushed and my eyelashes are bothering my face.

"I'm fine," I say. "I just don't like people to know every single thing about me. And I thought that was sort of obvious, but maybe not. Anyway, it's complicated and you guys probably wouldn't really get it."

"Help us get it," Maddy says, and she leans forward like she really means it. I try to tell myself that Maddy is my friend too. That she's maybe even my second-best friend and that it's nice to have more than one best friend. Maybe what Dad says is wrong. I don't have to be lonely to be special. So I try.

"My dad—" I start. I pull his sweater more tightly around me. It's soft in some parts and scratchy in others and I hope he never asks for it back. "It matters," I say, "to be good with magic."

"Everyone knows that," Maddy says with a shake of her head that tells me she doesn't get it at all, just like I knew she wouldn't.

"I'm about to be very magical," I say. "So we have to be careful."

"Maybe I'll be very magical too," Maddy says. She

shrugs. "Maybe I've worked hard enough, maybe you're just Rose Alice Anders, and not Little Luck, and that's the story that reporter's going to write." When Maddy's done talking, she looks up at the sky before looking back at me. She raises her eyebrows, which I guess means she wants a response, but there's no response to what she's said. Maddy turns to Ginger with an expectant look, her mouth a little open, her eyes blinking a few extra times.

That look again. That, and a tiny movement she makes with her head. A jut or a jerk or a *something*, and I don't understand anything at all except for one really big thing, which is that Ginger and Maddy have talked about this before, have talked about *me* before, and I wouldn't really like what they've been saying.

I wait for Ginger to disagree with Maddy or to stand up for me or to somehow undo that jut of Maddy's head, that code that isn't a code at all, that thing that's right in front of me.

Ginger sort of shuffles her feet. She clears her throat. It almost seems like she's going to say something, but then she just . . . doesn't.

And I don't either. Because there isn't really anything to say.

I'm Rose Alice Anders, Little Luck, the girl who's destined to be magical, who everyone knows is going capture more magic than any other new twelve-year-old capturer.

I don't know what Ginger and Maddy have been saying about me, but that's the truest true thing, and nothing they say can change that.

"We'll all get the magic we're meant to get," I say. I reach for my dad's words. And his confidence. "I know magic is hard to understand, but you'll see when you're there. You'll understand. What's supposed to happen happens, because magic says so."

The words feel good to me, but I don't see Maddy's face change.

"Right, Ginger?" I say. She's heard my dad say it almost as often as I have. She gives a little nod. "*Right?*" I say again, because I know she agrees, and I know she shouldn't side with Maddy over me, especially not right now, at the most important moment of our lives.

"Sure, Rose," Ginger says.

"Sure, Rose," Maddy parrots. I try not to hear the particular tone they're using.

"We should keep practicing with the bubbles," I say, even though I'm not really in the mood anymore.

"I'm tired," Ginger says.

"Me too," Maddy says.

"Come on," I say, "it's about to be my birthday. And then it's about to be the most important day of my life."

"All our lives, I thought," Ginger says.

"Yes, right, of course, all our lives," I say. And part of me even wants it to be true. Because if all of our lives change, then Dad will be wrong and I won't have to be special and magical and lonely and like him.

I try to unthink the thought, but thoughts don't work that way. Even if I had magic, I'd be stuck with it. Because even very powerful magic, the kind my dad can capture but almost no one else ever gets ahold of, can get rid of some memories, but none of it can change thoughts or feelings.

I sometimes wish it could.

Seven

I turn twelve at 11:57 p.m. on December 31. We stay up for it every year and drink warm apple cider and talk about how the night I was born Dad had to leave the hospital in a hurry to get to TooBlue Lake. He made it out to his car when he remembered that an Anders baby, especially one born on New Year's Eve, should see some magic her first day on earth, so he drove home in a hurry and grabbed a jar Lyle had liked playing with because inside there was one strand of yellow light that looked a little like a laser, if you thought about it hard enough. Lyle was three at the time, and liked lasers, and jars, and lights, and playing with things that no one else thought he was supposed to be playing with.

Dad ran that jar all the way back to our little room at the hospital and opened it up. It opened easily, he said, and the beam of light sort of danced out and broke apart as magic always does. It was a silly magic, not the sort of thing he would have chosen for my first taste of magic if he'd thought about it, but he hadn't had time to think. So instead he'd chosen Lyle's favorite jar, which just happened to hold a magic that made everyone levitate one and a half inches off the ground for exactly three hours. It was a precise and absurd magic, which the bright, single beams of magic often are.

So I spent the first few hours of my life being held by my floating mother and worried over by floating nurses who had been close enough to breathe in a bit of the magic.

Dad had a good laugh on his drive to TooBlue Lake, wishing he'd chosen a more serious, deliberate magic, but also happy he'd chosen that exact one.

Then he caught his one hundred sixty-one jars of magic.

When Mom and Dad finish telling the story tonight, it's past midnight, which means it's New Year's Day, which means it's about time I got ready for my first magic capturing. I am still UnTired, so I won't be sleeping. None of us will. Dad says the UnTired will last until we are home from the capturing, and then we'll all sleep a nice, proud, contented sleep. I wonder again how it isn't breaking the rules, to be UnTired for the capturing, but I know better than to ask Dad about it.

He doesn't like being asked those kinds of questions.

I think instead of his instructions about what to do and when and how and the promise that Dad keeps repeating that I'll be *fine, no, better than fine, wonderful, the best ever, better than him.*

We watch an old movie about love and we play three rounds of Uno.

At four in the morning, I do one more round of firefly catching, one more lap around the house, one more session of sitting on the ground and listening to magic.

Correction: trying very hard to hear magic.

"It's even closer tonight, right, Rose?" Dad says. He breathes in really hard from his nose like he can smell it, too.

I listen. I listen and listen and listen and listen. I hear crickets and Lyle reading to himself in his room above us and Mom's knitting needles clickety-clacking against each other. I hear cars driving around on a highway outside of town and things rustling in the leaves of the Belling Bright Woods, which surround us on all sides.

I hear a lot.

I do not hear magic.

"Much closer," I say anyway, because I am Little Luck and maybe I just don't understand what magic sounds like; maybe it sounds like knitting needles and my brother's reading voice and a cricket. Maybe Dad described it wrong.

Maybe I am hearing it right now; I must be hearing it right now; I *must* be.

When we are done listening, Dad pulls me close to him. The sweater he's wearing today is blue and has holes in it. His scarf is black and reaches his knees. "Happy birthday," he whispers even though there's no reason to be quiet; we are alone. "I've been waiting for this day for twelve years." I can hear his smile. It makes me smile.

"Me too," I say. Maybe he can hear my smile, too. I hope so.

We go back inside and Mom's laid out plum and tomato salad and a bunch of slices of butter-soaked bread. It's Dad's lucky meal, the slapdash thing he put together when he was heading out the door to get Mom to the hospital to have me. They were low on everything because Mom had been ravenous the day before, eating all the sliced meat and bananas and cookies and cheeses they had around. So Dad cut up plums and tomatoes, warmed up some butter on the stove, let it turn to a thick, salty pool, and dipped two big pieces of bread in it. And that's what they ate on the way to the hospital, Mom taking tiny bites in between yelps and feeding Dad bites as he drove, and now it's meant to bring me luck.

Except I'm not supposed to need luck. I am the luck. If Dad says it, it must be true.

The meal tastes good: familiar and strange, a thing that no one eats but us. Lyle lumbers downstairs in his pajamas and takes a plate of it too, like he always does on my birthday. He doesn't comment on the taste, he doesn't comment on the reason for the meal, but he eats the whole thing up.

This is a lot of what Lyle and I are like with each other. Quiet, but knowing the same things. Not talking but together. Dad says we aren't alike at all, but he doesn't have any siblings, or any family at all really, so maybe he doesn't know what it is to see the same things in the same house and sit in all that knowing together.

"Big day," Lyle says when he's taken his bite, like he needed the food to get the words out. I'm about to make fun of him for wearing pajamas when he knew he wasn't going to be sleeping, but it feels like a joke someone's already made, a joke that doesn't need to be made, so I let it go.

"Yep," I say instead. "Big, big day."

And it does feel big. Bigger than I thought it would. But I feel small inside it, and that's the part I wasn't exactly waiting for.

Eight

We are on the bus before dawn.

As usual, Maddy won't let even a minute of silence stand between us. I'm on one side of her and Ginger's on the other, and we're right up front, just like we planned. Just like Ginger and I planned. I hadn't imagined Maddy would be with us, but here she is, too chatty with excitement and listing everything she ate this morning. Ginger nods like she cares, so I try to care.

"Oh, oatmeal, cool," I say, but even I don't believe me. "We have a special thing we eat every year—"

"We know," Maddy says. "You always have a special thing you do or say or eat." Maddy talks so fast that I sometimes can't keep up, can't tell if she's said something mean or matter-of-fact or friendly.

But this time she doesn't sound very friendly.

"Happy birthday, by the way," Ginger says, and that's when I realize that she didn't call me yesterday, on my actual birthday. We didn't eat ice cream in my living room and we didn't paint our nails with glittery polish and we didn't convince my father to open up a special birthday jar. We didn't do any of the things we do every other year, and I hadn't even thought to miss them.

But now I do. It's fast and powerful and I look to see if Ginger is feeling it too—the shock of forgetting, the gasp of missing. She's looking out the window. Her shoulders are relaxed. She doesn't remember forgetting to do all the things we've always done, and that makes me dizzy.

I look out the window too. We're driving through the Belling Bright Woods, which I love, which Dad loves, because they were grown entirely by magic. Magical seeds and magical flowers and magical roots of magical trees. It means some of the growth is unexpected colors and shapes and some of the flowers do strange things like sing or flutter their leaves or smell like bacon. On good days, Dad and I spend hours in these woods, marveling at what we find, adding little bits of magic ourselves.

Because it's all made from magic, sometimes something vanishes from the woods. Not any of the tall oak trees that were built from very powerful, long-lasting magic. But a bush, a patch of sparkly dirt, a collection of magical flowers. When magic is worn out, it simply stops, and that's part of what makes it so valuable and important. That's why it matters, how much we all capture.

Nothing about this morning is right. I want to start it over, the way it was supposed to be.

They take us in our regular old school buses, and I've always wondered if that's what they do in other towns traveling to other lakes to capture other jars of magic. We haven't read about it in our Global Studies class yet.

Then I think about the towns without magic, and what they do on New Year's Day. Ms. Flynn told us about noise-makers and sparklers and the things people in those towns have that sort of look and sound like magic but aren't magic at all.

I can't imagine living in a place where a tiny flame on a stick is the most magic you can muster. It's like trying to imagine a place without daylight or air or love.

"I want to get ten jars," Maddy says, continuing a train of thought I haven't been following. I wish it was Ginger next to me, but Maddy has a way of always getting the right seat at the right time. "I guess nine would be okay. Or eight. Maybe seven. But not six. Six jars is like nothing. Only two people got six jars or less last year, and those two people were Jamie Ollander and Victor Vase. I don't want to be like Jamie Ollander and Victor Vase. Jamie never washes her hair and Victor can barely speak above a whisper and they're both—well. I know we're supposed to focus on everyone's good parts, but let's just say that's really hard when it comes to Jamie Ollander and Victor Vase." Maddy shrugs. When Maddy shrugs, it means she's finished her thought and wants you to reply.

"I like Jamie Ollander," I say at last. Her younger sister is sitting in the front of the bus and I don't want her to overhear us. But also, I *do* like her, and I've never noticed her dirty hair, and Maddy's not exactly perfect, and even when she's stealing my seat or talking to reporters about me, I still don't comment on her hair or the sound of her voice. "I thought everyone liked Jamie Ollander."

"Not anymore," Maddy says, like she's got the most up-to-date version of some book I forgot to read. If I'm being totally honest, I'd rather Jamie Ollander were sitting next to me right now, with her supposedly dirty hair and six jars of magic. "She got new sneakers, as if that will fix everything."

Maddy herself is wearing new sneakers, red-and-purple ones. They're the kind everyone says help you move fast and jump high and capture more magic than you could with regular sneakers. I don't point Maddy's sneakers out to her. She knows what's on her feet, after all.

I look at my feet. My same old blue sneakers that I've had for a year and are a little too small, so my toes always hurt after a day of wearing them.

I asked Dad about all the special accessories my class-mates have. Even Ginger has a pair of gloves with rubbery fingertips, so that not a single whisper of magic could slip away from her. She got her glasses prescription rechecked and her new frames are black and sturdy and come complete with a band that ties around the back of her head to keep them from slipping.

Other kids have fancy lightweight jars and hats with beams of light attached to help them look in dark spaces, or they drink certain kinds of protein drinks for months before New Year's Day.

Dad shook his head at all of it.

"You can't take the magic out of magic," he said. "They've lost sight of how this all works. We find magic, and magic finds us. Magic tells us who we are. Who we are meant to be. You can't buy your way into that. You and I—we know better. We have our bare feet. Our fast hands. Our big hearts."

He put his hand over his heart, so I did the same.

"You're meant to capture magic," he said. "It's all right here." He tapped his hand against his shirt, like the beat of his heart had made its way outside his body, into his fin-gertips. I did the same and he smiled. "My bighearted girl," he said, his eyes a little teary with pride. I blushed a happy blush. Sometimes, Dad could see me just as clearly as he could see magic, and that was its own kind of magic. The best kind, actually.

"My ankle hurts," Ginger says, interrupting all my thoughts.

"I told you not to play soccer this year," Maddy says. "Not your first year capturing. Not any year, probably. Soccer is for little kids who can't capture magic. We have responsibilities now." Maddy sounds like her mother, like dozens of mothers and fathers who we know but try to ignore. There are two kinds of families, and Maddy's family is the first kind. The kind that thinks they can outsmart the rest of us and get magic that way. By quitting soccer and buying fancy shoes and thinking about nothing else. Maybe that's how it was in their old town. But not in Belling Bright. "It's *magic*," Maddy says. "I mean. *Magic*. You have to do everything you can to get as much as you possibly can. You have to *try*."

I shake my head. Maddy doesn't get it. She can try as hard as she wants—magic knows who she is, what's in her heart, what kind of person she is. Magic knew my dad was special. It will know whether Maddy is.

It will know whether I am, too.

Sometimes I wonder why magic chose my dad. Then I think about his booming voice and wide smile and how it feels when the whole of him is focused on me. He's a fire— the closer you are to him, the warmer you feel. The brighter he becomes.

The more powerful.

I try to feel like a fire, too. Or even a flame. I'd settle for a non-magical New Year's Eve sparkler.

I'm not sure I can burn so bright. But I'll try. "Soccer is really important to Ginger. Plus, she's amazing at it," I say.

I look at Ginger and wait for her to weigh in. But she doesn't, so I look at her even more closely. It's more than her new glasses, more than her fancy gloves. Her jaw is set a particular way that I don't recognize. She's tapping her feet on the bus's floor, and when I look down at the busy beat I see it's footwork she's practicing. In brand-new red-and-purple sneakers. The kind that are supposed to make you run fast and jump high. The kind that Maddy's wearing. Ginger sees me seeing them and tucks them under the seat in front of her.

"Anyway," I say, "Ginger would never quit."

Maddy raises her eyebrows and we both wait for Ginger to reply. She should be agreeing with me swiftly, easily. Ginger wants to be a soccer star when she grows up, and it's possible. She's better than anyone in our grade, better than my brother, Lyle, better than any of his friends—I swear she's even better than some of the people she makes me watch on TV after school when I'd rather be drawing pictures of the kids in our class, the things we ate for lunch, the toys strewn all over Ginger's house.

It's a long, long time before Ginger replies. And when

she does, I barely recognize her. "I could give up soccer," she says. "You know, if I had to."

"Told you," Maddy says. She's never looked prouder. She flips hair that isn't there behind her shoulder, forgetting that the whole perfect blond bunch of it is all tied up in elaborate braids.

"If you had to?" I say. "Why in the world would you have to?"

"We're not all like you, Rose," Ginger says. "You've got natural—it's going to be easy for you. My family really needs more magic. With all of us kids. And my dad gone. And—yeah. We need to try. I know what your dad says. That there's no trying, that it's all—that some people are just meant for more magic than other people. But not everyone agrees with every single thing your dad says about magic."

"Or anything else," Maddy says, and she shrugs and half smiles and I guess it's possible to know something and not know it at the same time, because I don't know what she's trying to say right now. But I also sort of do.

"You don't know anything about my dad," I say, but they both pretend not to hear me.

"I need to get at least ten jars, like Maddy," Ginger says. "I—I don't want to be like Jamie and Victor either. And soccer isn't—it's just kicking a ball around. It's not important. Magic is what's important."

"Ginger—" I start, but I don't know where I'm going, so

56

I stop. "You love soccer," I say at last.

"I don't want to talk about it."

"We talk about everything. If you had some whole new brain you should have told me."

"I tried."

I don't know what she means by that. I see Ginger every day. We have a sleepover every weekend. If she had something to tell me, it would be easy. She could just tell me. She wouldn't need to *try* to tell me.

"We can talk now," I say.

"No," Ginger says. "We can't." She points at the view in front of us. TooBlue Lake, bigger than I remembered, bluer too. Surrounded by tall trees and dotted with glints of sunlight. I remember what my father told me about those glints. That they're the best kind of magic to capture, the most beautiful, the most rare.

He told me that only the very best capturers can trap those bits of sunlight in their jars.

He told me I could do it. So I will.

Nine

Our bus is the first to arrive. They give the new twelve-year-olds the most time by the lake. A head start. But only barely. In a few minutes, everyone else will arrive. But for right now, Maddy, Ginger, and I stand with our twenty-two classmates and take in the size of the lake, the feel of the ground underfoot, the temperature, the scope of what we are meant to do.

I close my eyes like my father taught me. And I listen.

There are the easy sounds: Ginger's breathing next to me. She has a tiny wheeze in her breath from years of asthma, and I love how it marks her as herself, how I could follow something as simple as her breath to find her. I hear

Maddy tapping her fingers on her thigh, counting glints on the lake or leaves in the trees or blades of grass. Anything could be magic, and she knows it.

Dad says that while capturing magic, some people scoop up everything they can get their hands on and see what it is later. "They come back with who knows what," he told me during one of our recent late nights trying to distinguish stars from planets in the sky, since an attention to detail is part of capturing magic successfully. "Old pennies. Dirt. Toilet water. The kind of dust you find on the highest shelf of a bookcase. These people. They come in with jars of junk and ask if it's magic. No instincts."

He said *no instincts* the same way he said *these people* and *junk*. Words that tasted all kinds of lemon-sour, coffee-bitter, undesirable.

"It's a good thing people like that don't get much magic. Don't get powerful magic. They wouldn't know what to do with it. They'd try for a sunny day and open a magic that turned them invisible. They'd want to cure their cold and end up using magic that lengthens minutes into hours. Magic wouldn't let that happen. Magic goes where it's meant to go, to people who know what to do with it."

"So why do we have to practice looking at the planets?" I asked. "Why do we practice with the fireflies? And the running?" It's a question I had thought a hundred times over the years. If everything is the way my dad says, why practice at all? Why study? Why not just trust the magic will come?

"We're showing magic we're ready for it. We're making ourselves open to it. The magic can't do all the work. We have to show up and let it know we're prepared." Dad whispered the words. It felt like a secret, something he was only sharing with me. He was so calm and so sure and he made it all sound so beautiful. I leaned against him a little and he wrapped an arm around my shoulder.

"Oh," I said, wanting to understand everything as clearly as he did. "I get it."

"I knew you would, Little Luck," Dad said, and my heart was so bright from the way he saw me. The way he believed in me.

Now it's New Year's Day, so I listen as hard as I can for magic, for answers, for my destiny. I have to do better than hearing Ginger's and Maddy's breaths and hearts and wiggling fingers and nervous toes. I hear those things all the time.

Beyond their breathing and tapping there's the sound of little lake waves hitting the shore and the breeze running through the branches. But those sounds are easy too. Anyone could hear them.

I think I hear the scuttle of a small animal digging and the door of one of the cabins way up the hill opening, then closing. It's possible another bus is getting close. Maybe I can hear tires on a dirt road a mile away.

But none of that is magic.

When I open my eyes again, Maddy is polishing her glass jars and Ginger is looking around and taking notes.

I don't have a notebook. And I don't have anything to polish jars with. Dad said I wouldn't need anything like that.

"When do we start?" I ask.

"I think we already have," Ginger says.

I should have heard it but didn't. The sound of a few of our classmates—mostly boys, mostly strong-shouldered, mostly the kind who talk back to teachers and ask why I don't ever wear dresses—have already sprinted off to the hills. They're picking cabins and planning trails and charting treetops to get a sense of where the best magic might be.

"Don't bother with a cabin," Dad told me last night when I asked if the mattresses were comfortable, if people wore pajamas or slept in their clothes. "You won't be sleeping."

"I get tired," I said.

"You won't be tired," Dad reminded me. "You'll be UnTired. You'll be ready. Your whole self will turn toward the magic. You'll see."

He sounded so sure I almost forgot all my other questions.

Maybe I didn't need to ask them anyway. I'm lucky to

have him looking out for me. To have him teaching me how to listen for magic and capture it and make it my own. I'm lucky that he does what needs to be done.

Even when I don't understand it.

"And when it's all done, I can rest. And have the feast," I said, because thinking about bacon and pancakes helps me forget about other things, like the way Dad sometimes makes me feel or the things he's said to Mom when he thinks I haven't been listening or how sometimes all the things he says about magic don't add up in my mind, but I was never very good at math anyway, so that must be why.

Tomorrow morning, there will be a breakfast feast right here where we're standing. I've heard the pancakes are so good you can't ever enjoy regular pancakes again. I've heard there are fluffy eggs and platters of cheese and fruit so sweet it tastes like candy and hot chocolate that is just hot fudge sauce in a giant ceramic mug. I wish we were there now and could skip this next part.

It surprises me, feeling that way.

"Let's go pick a spot," Ginger says now. Almost everyone but us has started moving.

"Let's get the closest cabin," Maddy says. "Everyone else will be trying to get all the way up the hill, since the view is so nice. Let's get the one closest to the lake." I can tell from the fake-casual way she says it that she's been planning this forever but wants to pretend it's a brand-new thought. I've seen her do this before. Maddy plans everything—who she will talk to at recess, what comment she'll make about *The Giver* when we discuss it in class, how she'll wear her hair for New Year's Day magic capturing. But she likes all of it to look easy and accidental and natural. As if she doesn't have to try at all.

I'm waiting for it to be easy. Nothing feels very easy right now. Not even being with my friends.

There's a shout and a whoop and a holler from up at the top of the hill.

"He's got it!" someone calls, their voice echoing against our nervous silence. "The First Magic!"

I wonder if Ginger's and Maddy's hearts sommersault the way mine does. Sometimes the First Magic isn't caught for an hour. Usually it's at least twenty minutes. But news travels down the hill at the speed of light, and we learn that the First Magic was caught by Evan Dell, who is the tallest boy in the grade and, according to me and Ginger and Maddy, the cutest too.

I picture Dad in my head, rolling his eyes. *Beginner's luck*, Dad would say. *The First Magic isn't the best magic. It's not the most magic. It's just the First Magic.*

Still, I wanted it to be mine. The First Magic is extra bright; it lights up your jar and turns different colors depending on the time of day, as if you captured a bit of sky.

I would have liked to set a bit of sky on our mantel, in between the jar filled with starlight and the one with a bit of a tree's long shadow trapped inside. I would have liked to sit with my father and watch it turn from orange to blue to black to gray to yellow. I would have liked to capture the First Magic so I could know, for sure, that I'm who my father has promised me that I am.

My father knows everything about magic, and he knows that I am ready for big magic. So it must be true. It has to be. I just have to do what he's told me, be who he's asked me to be. Little Luck. Rose Alice Anders. A girl who is about to capture more magic than any other twelve-year-old has.

"You guys get a cabin," I say, sticking my chin a little into the air, straightening my shoulders so that I look as strong and sure as those boys who didn't hesitate to run up the hill. "I won't be sleeping."

I sit on the ground and take off my shoes, untying one, then the other. I don't exactly want to. It's cold out and the ground is covered in pebbles that will hurt the bottoms of my feet. But I promised my father I would, and I have to be something more than a person who is standing at the bottom of the hill, hearing about Evan Dell's success. I have to become the person I am destined to be.

"I thought it would be fun," Ginger says, "the three of us rooming together. Like a sleepover."

"I thought you have to give up everything fun so that you can capture all the magic you need."

"Rose," Ginger says. "I'm allowed to try. I'm allowed to do it my way."

"Dad says trying is the opposite of magic," I say. It's not something Dad's really said, not exactly, but close enough. I don't like the way Ginger's looking at my bare feet, like they're weird and maybe even gross and almost as bad as Jamie Ollander's unwashed hair. I don't like that she's had all these thoughts and feelings that I haven't known about.

"What are you doing with the bare feet? Isn't that trying?" Ginger asks.

"You don't understand—" I start, and I want to tell her about last week, when I asked if I really had to go barefoot for New Year's Day. I want to tell her that Dad's shoulders tensed and he slammed the front door and Lyle made me promise to go barefoot whenever Dad said to go barefoot. I want to tell her that I don't understand everything my dad says and does either, but that he is Wendell Anders and he's magical and special and the best person in all of Belling Bright, so it doesn't matter if I understand or not. I want to tell her yes, I do whatever my dad does, whatever he says to do, and it's impossible to imagine doing things any other way. But I don't say any of that. I don't let myself.

"You're right," Ginger says. "I don't understand you at all right now."

"Come on," Maddy says. "Let's just go. We knew this might happen."

It's that word—*we*—that changes everything. It's been a bad morning, but Maddy saying *we* makes it worse. Ginger and *I* are supposed to be the *we*. Maddy is the extra person, the tagalong, the sort of friend who is supposed to be decidedly outside our *we*.

My throat closes up. But I can't care about any of that. I have to find my magic. Or let it find me.

"I really can't have the distraction of you two anyway," I say to the shape of their bodies leaning a little toward one another and away from me. I say it to the way that Ginger's shoes match Maddy's and the way she's looking at me now, like she feels bad for me. I say it to the jar at her side, which is open and ready for capturing, even though we promised I would open her first jar for capturing every year and she would open mine, the way we used to do when we were seven and eight and nine and playing New Year's Day. It was supposed to be our ritual, fitting right in with the way we make each other Valentine's Day cards every year and dress in identical outfits for the first day of school and spend our birthdays together.

Except not this year, I guess. Not anymore. Something vanished before I even had a chance to say goodbye to it, and it makes me sad, but more than sad it makes me angry. I want to stomp on her already open jar and all the promises and plans we've ever made.

Ginger sees me seeing her already open jar.

She doesn't say anything. She shrugs like I should have known it was coming.

But I didn't. I didn't know at all.

Ten

I don't feel very magical right now, but I know that Too-Blue Lake itself has more magic than practically anywhere else in the world and definitely more than anywhere else on this beach. Dad says it's where all the magic comes from. That it's brewed up in the lake and then lapped onto the shore and the breezes blow bits and pieces of it this way and that so that we have to go searching for it. But the most magic is right there in the lake. And if I could catch one of those glints of sunlight in a jar, it would be like catching ten regular jars of magic.

Dad also said to trust myself, that I am the luck, that I will know how to do it because I am meant to do it.

And that's what I have to believe, because that is what

has always been true. The lake is there, shining and blue, and all I know is I want to run away from Ginger and Maddy and their cabin and their plans and their stupid matching sneakers and the way they shrug at the things that matter to me. I roll my pants up past my knees so I can wade in. Later, adults will dive in, older kids will swim out to the other shore, and my classmates will maybe skim the shoreline looking for the kind of magic that gets lapped up in little lake waves.

But right now, TooBlue is mine. The magic there is slippery and sometimes impossible to get ahold of. It's for last-minute miracles, not for the early hours when magic is everywhere. But Dad says to follow my instincts, that they are good, like his, and my heart, which is pure and open and big like his. And my heart and my guts say *lake lake lake*, so I don't ignore them. I walk right up to the place where water meets sand and let it hit my toes for one second before walking in. It's so cold that if I hesitate I'll never do it at all, so I don't hesitate, I go all the way to my knees and I stick my jar in the water and bring it back up. And when it's out of the water, I look hopefully inside. It's pretty much impossible, to get lake magic on a first try, but I'm special, I'm Rose Alice Anders and my father is Wendell Anders and he captured one hundred sixty-one jars of magic because I was born, and everyone is waiting to see what my first year will bring, what my legacy means. Who I am.

I lift the jar of magic high above me. It's easier to see what you've got that way, my father says. Magic needs a little light on it, and the sun is bright enough to help now, so I hold the jar this way and that, looking for the flicker, the shimmer, the glint, the diamond of light that appears on the surface of the lake.

The jar is full. But not with magic. Just with lake water. TooBlue Lake has the prettiest water in the world. But there's a difference between beautiful and magical, and Rose Alice Anders is supposed to be able to tell the difference.

I dump the contents back into the lake and try again.

Dad says the best magic capturers are resilient. He calls it grit, and I call it hope, but it's all the same. It means you don't let one jar of lake water ruin your day.

I lower the jar back into the water and rush at a glint of sunlight sparkling in all that blue. I throw my whole body at it. Then I lift my jar to the sky and peer underneath.

Just lake water again.

More buses are rolling in, and cars behind them. Somewhere, Lyle and Mom and Dad are driving around a corner, seeing the sign for TooBlue Lake, wondering if I've caught the First Magic. It's too late for that, but I am positive that I will catch a bit of lake magic, I'll be the first one to do it, something that's never been done before by a kid who is only twelve.

I walk farther into the lake. My jeans get soaked. I walk all the way to my waist, and my mustard-colored hoodie isn't dry anymore either, but none of that matters; nothing matters except the jar and the glint and the magic I am about to proudly possess.

I skim my jar across the water, thinking about fireflies and heartbeats and Dad's lucky scarf around my neck and how much he loves me and my destiny to be Rose Alice Anders, the next great capturer of magic.

I do not think about Ginger and Maddy and their laughter as it peals across the lake's surface. I don't think, not even one little bit, about what will happen tomorrow and next week and next month if Ginger and Maddy are now best friends and I am not a best friend anymore. I don't think about the never hearing magic and the never feeling very magical and the always wondering why Dad has so much magic and Mom has so little and if any of that makes any sense.

I don't think about how I once whispered to Lyle, *Do you trust magic?* And how he didn't answer.

I don't think about how very very cold it is and how very very wet my clothes are.

I let my heart find the magic. And it does. I'm positive it does. I feel my heart surge and my eyes get a little weepy and my hands shake and I swear I can hear it now, *magic*. It's a hum and a whisper and the world's tiniest wind chime and it's beautiful. And it's mine.

I lift the jar into the sky. People have gathered along the shore. Kids in my class, but others too. Older kids. Parents. Teachers. I'm pretty sure I can see Lyle's long hair and Mom's sharp shoulders and Dad's scruffy beard.

"Lake magic!" I call out. I say it loud enough for my father to hear. I want him to be a part of this moment with me. I want him to know that I have believed everything he's ever told me, and I have the gift he promised I would have and that I am the greatest young capturer here on TooBlue Lake. I want him to see that magic found me, because I was worth finding. "I captured lake magic!" I say again, lifting my jar even higher up, even closer to the sun, so that the glint will reach shore, will bounce off the lake's surface and the sun's beams and really show itself off.

"Rose," my father calls back. I wait for his congratulations. Maybe he will run through the water to reach me, lift me into the air, kiss my hair. Maybe he will cry.

"I did it!" I call back.

"Rose," Dad says again, more stern this time. He isn't diving into the lake water, he isn't grinning from ear to ear. In fact, he doesn't look happy at all. "Look up," he says. "Like I taught you. Listen. Lunge. Look."

There's a chuckle from the crowd. The Anders family secret is that simple. Listen. Lunge. Look. Any of them could do it. Of course, if you believe my father, there's the fourth thing, which is luck and heart and being the kind of person who leans toward magic, being the kind of person who magic leans toward.

I am the kind of person that magic leans toward. I have to be. That is the story of the day I was born, and that has to be the story today.

I am Rose Alice Anders, and I am the first twelve-year-old to ever catch lake magic.

I look up at last.

The jar feels heavy, something I should have noticed before.

I look more closely. It is filled to the brim with water. It seems to be getting heavier by the moment. I turn it this way and that, searching for the telltale glint, the spark of something more than a jar full of water.

Magic is there or not there, Dad told me, back when I asked him how I would be able to tell if I'd caught magic or not. He walked me to our windowsill, to one of the many rows of jars in our home. He was right, of course. The magic was simply *there*. I couldn't have said what exactly it looked like—was it the extra-orangeness of a leaf or the almost-green of a drop of water? Was it a floating piece of glitter or the fuzz of a feather? Or was it something else entirely?

I didn't know. It didn't matter. I could tell the difference between a jar of magic and a jar of not-magic. Magic was there or not there.

And today, as I'm soaked in lake water, I can tell. Magic is not there. It's not here, in my jar. I didn't catch anything but a jar full of water.

That, and the sinking feeling that the map of my world, the list of things I was promised, is shifting as quickly as kids are running up and down the hill, as quickly as a firefly bats its wings against your hands, as quickly as any magic has ever moved.

Eleven

It is a long walk from the lake to the shore.

Long and wet and downward-gazing, because the idea of knowing who was on the shore watching my ridiculous performance is more than I can handle. It's enough to know my family was watching, and to suspect that most of my classmates were, too.

Mom covers me in a towel the second I reach her. "You must be cold," she says, which is nice, because it's what she would say in any circumstance where I've been standing in the water in the wintertime. It makes me feel almost normal. I'm still Rose Alice. I'm still her daughter. I'm still okay.

Except I'm not really okay. I'm shaking, first of all, and even though there are hours and hours and hours of New Year's Day to go, I don't want to be here. I don't want to try again. I've been waiting my whole life to capture magic, and I failed so spectacularly, the idea of trying again makes me sick.

"What were you thinking?" Lyle asks. He's blushing, like just being related to me is a humiliation.

"I thought I had it," I say.

Lyle rolls his eyes. "'Course you did," he says. "Rose Alice Anders. So magical she dives right into the water. As if there isn't easy magic right here in the sand, or stuck in between blades of grass." Lyle is only sarcastic when he's scared, so I guess he's scared. But I'm not sure of what.

I look around. He's gesturing all over the place, as if the magic is so obvious that I must see it too. But I can't seem to tell the difference between grass waving a little in the wind and grass thrumming with magic. Dad always said it would be obvious. When magic is stuffed in a jar, I can see it. But out here, at TooBlue Lake, all I see is a lake and the shore and the people of Belling Bright doing a million times better than me.

I look at Dad, but Dad's looking at the lake. He steps away from us, out of earshot, so I lean closer to Lyle. "Can you show me?" I ask.

"Show you what?" The crowd around us is starting to dissipate. They're heading to the cabins, up the hill, and to the edge of the lake. The air is punctuated with cries of success. Little bits of magic trapped in jars like it's nothing, like it's as easy as Dad said it would be.

"Show me where the magic is," I say.

Lyle squints and shakes his head. "Rose. What have you been studying all this time?"

"How to capture magic," I say. "Or, well, no. I've been practicing how to help the magic find me. Like it's supposed to. Right?"

"That's what Dad says," Lyle says. "That he has magic because he's supposed to have magic. That he gets powerful magic because he's worthy of it."

"Right," I say.

"Right," Lyle says. Sometimes I can say one word and Lyle can say one word but we're actually saying a thousand words.

"We trust the magic to know what it's doing," Lyle says. He waits for me to agree, and I know I have been taught exactly that, but it has always been hard to be sure about, hard to trust. I look at my big brother to see if it's hard for him too. If he wonders, the way I do, late at night and even right here and right now on the shores of TooBlue Lake.

I close my eyes. I listen for something, anything. Mostly I can hear kids laughing. I can hear Ginger's feet running away from the shore, and Maddy's squeals as she follows her. I can hear everything changing and my friendships breaking apart and my heart beating out its rhythm of worry and confusion. I can hear Lyle moving from embarrassment to annoyance to pity.

I can hear Dad coming back to us, whispering to Mom, but I can't hear what he's saying.

I open my eyes and look up at Lyle. It's what I do when I don't know what else to do. Sometimes Lyle is the brother who makes up limericks about how annoying I am or pretends he can't hear me even when I'm right next to him, talking directly into his ear.

But other times he is the person who sits next to me on the bit of slanted roof outside my bedroom window and distracts me from whatever is happening inside our house. Sometimes, Lyle is the only person who knows anything about me at all.

Right now, he is that person.

"It's like a shadow," Lyle says. "Or like when you think you see something out of the corner of your eye, but when you turn to look at it head-on, it's not there. Magic's like that. You can't look at it head-on."

I nod. Dad never tried explaining any of this to me. I guess he didn't think it was necessary.

"It's from the heart," Dad says, joining us again, interrupting the thing between Lyle and me, and I can practically hear the bubble we were in pop, a sound louder and clearer and more sure than any whisper of magic. "There's no tricks. You open your heart, and it's there." His voice is gruff. He's still only looking at the lake and not at me at all. "Or not there. Whatever magic thinks is best."

The silence after this sentence lasts forever. I get lost in it.

"I opened up my heart and that's why I went into the lake," I say. I want it to be true, but it isn't. It was from my head. It was from a sureness. Not sureness that magic was in the lake, though. Sureness that I was meant for something big. Sureness that I would show them all. Sureness that I could be Little Luck, and sureness that I had to be Little Luck.

Dad shakes his head. "That wasn't magic, Rose. Whatever you felt. That wasn't it." His face is a hard knot of anger.

"You said it would be easy," I say. My voice is starting to shake. All of me is starting to shake. "So I thought it would be easy."

Dad doesn't reply. Doesn't move. Everyone else has now run this way and that, so it's just my little family still standing here, trying to unremember what just happened.

"Tell her to get back out there," Mom says. "She needs to try again."

"Go back out there," Dad says, but it sounds like nothing, like the kind of thing he'd say to anyone—Lyle, the mail carrier, a porcupine, a lampshade.

"Okay," I say, even though it's the last thing I want to do and even though it feels completely impossible.

"Tell her she can do it," Lyle says. He and Mom are so much alike, and I don't think I knew it until right now, because Mom doesn't play video games and Lyle doesn't run a daycare; Mom doesn't eat pizza cold in the mornings and Lyle doesn't wear his hair in a loose bun on the tip-top of his head. But underneath all of that, they are the same.

They love me the same.

Dad loves me too. But it's different.

I don't think it's supposed to be so different.

"I have work to do," Dad says. "We need magic. I don't have time for all this. Not today."

"Wendell," Mom says, a little bit of warning in her voice, the way she sometimes talks to a toddler who is smearing paint in his hair or banging toy cars against the floor.

"I suggest you all get to work," Dad says, not looking at any of us now, just at the trees and the magic he's ready to capture.

And he does capture it. Within a few minutes he's filled four jars of magic, and he's sprinting up the hill to catch a fifth. I don't see what it is he's chasing. I don't see the magic or hear it or know it's around at all.

I put my shoes back on. My sneakers are the beat-up pale blue canvas kind, not the fancy red-and-purple kind made for jumping and leaping.

"Just try to get at least a couple jars. Easy ones," Lyle says before he bounds off too, joining up with a group of kids his age who seem to be into New Year's Day more for the jokes and fun and partying than for the magic.

Mom kisses my forehead. "Don't worry about a thing," she says. She doesn't tell me I will certainly catch magic soon. She doesn't tell me it doesn't matter, what I did in the lake.

She doesn't even tell me that she's going to leave me there, so she can walk off to capture her own magic. She's simply there one minute and gone the next, tiptoeing up by the rocks, as nimble and graceful as anyone.

My shoes hurt, my pants are soaking wet, my hair's in my eyes, and I'm still holding a jar of lake water like it's magic, like it's something, like I'm special. But it isn't, it isn't, I'm not.

I'm not.

Twelve

I *try to* remember lessons from Dad. They all started out nice and clear and sturdy: *take your shoes off and feel the earth, listen for tiny chimes and whispers of air, don't worry about anyone else, you'll be fine, you're a natural, you're special, the magic will find you.*

The magic finds the people who deserve it.

I walk away, as far away as I can from the thing that happened, and I find myself at the top of the hill, the very very top, past the cabins and the patches of flowers where I'm certain magic is probably lurking. I walk past my classmates and their snickers, past everyone who hoped I wouldn't do well or was positive I would, past all of them and the things they've thought about me and whispered about me and wondered about me.

I walk until I'm all alone.

And Dad said being special was lonely, but he didn't say that finding out you're maybe not special at all would be lonely too.

When Dad said I might be lonely, he didn't say it like it mattered, like it would hurt. He said it like it was fine, and maybe that's how it feels to him, because when I think about it, I've never seen my dad have many friends. I've never watched people try to become his friend, even. People mostly stay away from Dad and lean close to Mom and that's how it's really always been. At holiday parties and school events and even right now, as I watch them take a break to drink some water with Ginger's mom and Maddy's dad, that's how it is. Bodies are leaning toward Mom. Women touch her arm sometimes and men nod and laugh at the things she says. She doesn't seem to notice. Her face is tilted toward my father, and his face is looking somewhere else entirely, somewhere far away. Sometimes his hand will reach out and circle her arm or squeeze her shoulder.

And when it does, sometimes, but not always, Mom's fingers will fold into her palms or her shoulders will move a tiny bit, as if her heartbeat has temporarily relocated to her extremities for one powerful *bah-dum* before making its way back to where it's supposed to be.

That's what it does right now, when his hand finds its way to rest near her neck, a place I don't like watching his hand be. Mom's shoulders jump, Dad's hand stays, and I am here wondering if he was wrong about me, and if that means he could be wrong about so many other things. No one standing with them is saying anything, but all of them are leaning a little farther away, and maybe I don't see magic very well, but I see other things, important things, things I have been trying not to see.

I should be looking for magic, but I'm not.

Instead I am seeing even the shallow breaths my mother is taking and I'm hearing her shift her weight from one hip to another and I'm thinking if I could see the magic the way I can see her discomfort, I wouldn't be in this moment to begin with.

And wouldn't that be something.

Thirteen

A Story I Am Thinking About
on the Top of This Hill

Once, Ginger and I stole a jar of magic.

It was Ginger's idea. She talked about wanting to do it once a day, for ten days, and then we did it, because I didn't think I could have the same conversation eleven times in a row.

It wasn't like Ginger to break rules. She didn't even like staying up past bedtime, let alone stealing something valuable from my parents. But it *was* like Ginger to get something into her head and be totally unable to let it go.

And it was like Ginger to try to fix something complicated by doing something simple. The complicated thing was my parents fighting downstairs while we were trying to watch *The Sound of Music* upstairs in the playroom for the millionth time. And the simple thing was to fix it by using magic.

"That's what it's *for*," Ginger said the first time she brought it up. Julie Andrews was singing about deer and rain and sewing and I was doing everything I could to listen to that instead of my mother's almost-weeping voice and my dad's hand hitting the table a little too hard at the ends of his sentences.

"You think magic is for stealing?" I asked.

"It's for fixing things," she said. "Cars. Broken windows. Illnesses. Families."

"My family doesn't need fixing," I said, and it sounded true enough, but Ginger shook her head like she didn't believe me.

The next day, my parents fought outside the school, on their way in to our choir performance. Maddy heard them and reported it to me and Ginger, and we watched them from the window in the girls' bathroom. My dad's arms waved around and my mother's stayed locked together in front of her, and the two of them whisper-yelled until it was time to come inside and watch Maddy, Ginger, and me sing a bunch of songs about how great it is when the seasons change.

Ginger raised her eyebrows and wiggled them around

before telling me again that she knew how to fix it.

My parents fought at my tenth birthday party, the one we had in the middle of December at the roller-skating rink where there was supposed to be a fortune-teller and a cotton candy machine but all that was actually there were a bunch of smelly socks and a guy who sold stale pretzels and the sound of my father telling my mother she was *wrong* and *absurd* and the sound of my mother driving away with their car, so that Dad and I had to hitch a ride home with Ginger's family.

"Now?" Ginger asked before I got out of the car that day, and I wondered what her mom and my dad thought she was talking about. I shrugged instead of shaking my head, and I guess that's when her idea became our idea.

We talked about it for another week, until the day of her family's Christmas party, when my mother and father got into it outside the bathroom, where I guess they thought no one could hear them, but in fact absolutely everyone heard every word they said. I made sure no one *saw* them by standing at the corner where the hallway turns and leads you toward the bathroom.

It was important that even if every single person in all of Belling Bright could hear them, no one could see them.

I had only seen once. Or maybe two or three times, but it felt better to say it was only once.

"It's time," Ginger said when my parents' fight was over

and the party was continuing on as if it never happened, including my parents, who were holding hands and talking to whoever had the guts to talk to them. My father's hand looked like it was holding on tight. My mother's looked loose, like she couldn't quite convince herself to commit her fingers to holding on to his.

Ginger and I were eating cookies behind the Christmas tree and watching everyone from there, because we were sort of jokingly and sort of actually hiding from Maddy.

"I don't know," I said. "Maybe."

"They're here, so no one's at your place. No one will notice if we go. They haven't noticed we're missing right now, even. It's time."

"It's not that bad," I said, and even I knew it wasn't true.

"Do you want them to get divorced?" Ginger asked.

"Of course not."

"I heard your mom ask my mom about the houses in the middle of town."

The houses in the middle of town were very cute and very small and very neat and very perfect for parents who had split up. Maddy's dad lived in one, and Lyle had a friend with two dads who split up and now lived next to each other in the houses in the middle of town. Every once in a while a friend would have a birthday party at one of those houses, and it was always a friend with divorced parents, and there were always way more presents than my birthdays, and usually it seemed like everything was fine but maybe a little more confusing and sometimes a little sadder and I'd always wonder what it was like before, when the whole family lived in another house, on the edge of town instead of right there in the center.

"That's not true," I said to Ginger, but I was pretty sure Ginger wasn't a liar.

"It is true," Ginger said. "But we can fix it."

It struck me as odd that my parents wouldn't use the magic themselves to fix whatever was wrong between them. Maybe that meant it wasn't that bad.

Or maybe, maybe, it meant that it was so bad they didn't even think magic could fix it.

"Okay," I said. "We can try."

It was as easy as Ginger thought to sneak next door to my house and steal the jar of magic.

It took time to pick the perfect one. We looked in the back hall closet, at rows and rows of jars, all lined up neatly. They were different sizes and shapes and the magic inside came in all different colors and textures. Some glowed extra bright. Some were feathery or spiky or swirly. Each one was unique. I wanted the magic we chose to be forgettable but pretty, strong-looking but soft, too. I'd seen my dad choose jars for different things, and he couldn't ever explain how he knew one from the other, except that clear magic is usually about love and stretchy magic is about coming together and magic that glows is extra powerful. He chose a pebbly magic when Mom was sick one summer and a glittery magic when I was afraid of the dark. An airy, nearly invisible magic when Lyle was failing math class. A huge jar of watery magic the time the whole town came together to help a family who'd lost their home in a fire.

I needed to choose the right one.

Finally, after sifting through some very small jars with something cloudy inside, and a jar with little blades of grass, and one jar that had something orangey-yellow in it that looked like yarn, I chose a little bit of sunlight trapped in a narrow jar. The sunlight had some weight to it. That, and brightness, usually meant it was a magic that would last a while. It stretched from one side of the jar to the other, sticking to the sides.

"This?" I asked Ginger.

"That," Ginger said. It was the way we agreed to things—without discussion, just trying to see something the same way in the same moment. I loved that she saw that bit of stretchy, bendy, sunlight magic and knew the way I knew that it was what my parents, my family, needed. A little bit of sunshine. Something warm and easy and light let loose into our home.

We begged our parents to let Ginger stay over after her Christmas party, and we stayed up until everyone was asleep. In a few days it would be Christmas and I thought about cookies for breakfast and Mom leaning against Dad while we opened presents and Dad singing along with the radio and Mom saying how much she loved his voice, the way she used to do.

"Do you know how to do this?" Ginger asked. The two of us were sitting on the floor, the jar of magic between us. We stared it down, as if it could tell us what to do.

"I've seen my dad do it," I said.

"My mom usually does ours." Ginger touched the lid's top but didn't dare remove it.

"Lyle knows how to do it."

"Lyle? Really?"

Sometimes it feels like my family is a big rocky mountain I'm trying to climb, and Lyle is the rocks that jut out, the places where I can grab on to, the ledges that make it possible for me to keep climbing.

When Dad says something that doesn't seem like the kind of thing Dad should say, Lyle comes into my room and we sit on the roof and look at Belling Bright and all the people walking on the sidewalks and driving down the road. Mostly we don't talk. We throw acorns, trying to make them hit the highest branches on the big tree in our yard. We pretend it's a game we're choosing to play, and not one that we have to play because the house is too small for

Dad and all his feelings and us too.

The one thing we don't do is talk about Mom and Dad.

It's weird, I guess, because the rest of Belling Bright loves talking about my dad. Other towns, too. People everywhere know of Wendell Anders. They talk about his bare feet and his handsome smile and his booming voice. They say he's larger than life, and I hate when they say that, but I can't explain exactly why.

"It might be okay to ask for Lyle's help," I said. It was after midnight, which meant Mom and Dad were definitely asleep but Lyle might still be playing video games, sneaking chips into his room, laughing at some cartoon that seemed kind of stupid to me but made him happy.

"Your call," Ginger said. But I could tell from the tone of her voice that she didn't want him here, not really, and when Ginger wanted something it felt big and important to me. Always bigger and more important than whatever I might want.

I could tell from her posture (leaning) and the tone of her voice (choppy) that she wanted it to be just us opening this jar, and she wanted me to feel about my brother the way she feels about hers.

"You're right," I said. "Let's just do it you and I. We can figure it out. We've been watching people open up jars of magic our whole lives. How hard can it be?"

"Not hard at all," Ginger said. And she grabbed the jar of magic. I thought, since it was my family, that I'd be the one to open the jar and try to think the right thoughts to make the magic do the right thing. But Ginger didn't hesitate. She grunted, opening the jar, like the top was stuck on really tight.

"Stay together," she whispered, and I wasn't sure what she was picturing, but it definitely wasn't our old Christmas mornings or the way my dad looked at my mom in their wedding album pictures or that afternoon we spent hiking when Mom sprained her ankle and Dad carried her piggyback all the way home and Mom couldn't stop laughing and we all ate dinner in the living room so that Mom could keep her foot elevated on the couch.

"It's not exactly that I just want them to stay together—" I said, but Ginger put her hand on my knee and squeezed.

"Don't interrupt the magic," she said.

"Oh," I said. "Okay." But it didn't feel okay.

The little dot of sunshine escaped, we felt the tiniest shudder, and that was it. The magic had been let loose, and if all went well, if we'd picked the right jar, there would be no more fighting.

"I sort of thought I'd open the jar," I said to Ginger. "I thought maybe I'd try to do the magic."

"It was my idea," Ginger said.

"It's my family," I said. "And I'm—you know—I'm—"

"Little Luck," Ginger said. "I know. We all know. You're going to have a million chances to use all the magic you want. You're going to be able to do powerful, big stuff. Just this once, can't I do something that matters?"

I didn't know what to say. So I didn't say anything at all. I knew that worked sometimes, when people were mad. And it worked this time, like it worked all the other times.

Ginger and I were quiet for a while, and soon we were laughing together, then talking again, and it all felt good and familiar and like the way it had always been, except a little different too, because Ginger had used magic on my family and she hadn't done it the way I wanted and she'd looked at me like maybe being my best friend wasn't always so great, and like maybe she wished she could use some magic on me, too.

We stayed up until morning watching movies. By the time my parents found us we were zombie-eyed and humming Christmas carols and asking for cereal and toast and a nap.

And maybe the magic Ginger used worked, because Mom laughed at our sleepy faces and Dad poured us giant bowls of cereal and they didn't fight about any of it. They told us we could go back to bed until lunchtime, which we did. We fell asleep to the silence. Mom and Dad weren't fighting. The house was still. And Mom hasn't moved into a house in the center of town in the two years since.

So I guess it worked. They stayed together.

Except that's not quite exactly what was wrong to begin with. The thing I'm most scared of in my family was never that they might split up. It's that they might always stay together like this.

Fourteen

I am unmoving, on the top of my hill. I am watching everyone else so that I don't have to keep rewatching the images in my brain of what happened this morning. I see Ginger capture a few jars of magic and Maddy capture a few more. I see my father running this way and that, gathering up all the magic he possibly can. Mom captures magic in the exact opposite way, sort of wandering back and forth over the same spot until she sees something out of the corner of her eye.

I don't know what my method is. I thought it would be like Dad's, but I guess I'm actually just a girl who sits on the top of a hill and waits for magic to come to her. That's not exactly the kind of girl I wanted to be, but it seems like that's the only option left.

Day turns to evening and evening turns to night. Most people climb into cabins, and I can hear whispers that roll into laughter and laughter that quiets and shushes into whispers. The sounds of late-night friendship that I know well, but that are suddenly out of my reach. I try to listen for Ginger's laugh or Maddy's snores or *something* so that I can almost sort of pretend I'm in there with them and not up here alone.

Maybe I hear Ginger telling Maddy what to do with her jars of magic. Maybe I hear Maddy untying her shoes, sighing happily at beating me out as Ginger's best friend at last. I don't know. Maybe I just hear wind in the trees and Lyle and his friends howling at the moon as if they are wolves even though everyone knows they are not.

The only thing I don't hear is magic.

Night turns to early morning, and time is running out. When the sun is up, that's it. Magic capturing is over, the New Year will have begun, and I'll be the only one here without a single jar of magic to my name. No one's ever caught *nothing* before. Rose Alice Anders, the girl who was supposed to be the most magical, is actually the least, and now has no friends and maybe no family and might just stay at the top of this hill forever because what in the world else is she supposed to do?

I close my eyes. Not to hear magic, but just to sleep. I'm

exhausted, and the ground isn't exactly comfortable, but at least this patch of earth is mine for now and no one's watching me. At least I can hear crickets chirping and at least the moon is still in the sky, getting ready to vanish but not quite yet. If I fall asleep now, by the time I wake up the feast will have begun, and I don't think I can mess that up.

But right before I'm about to drift off, there's a breath on my shoulder and words in my ear.

"Try," the voice says.

I stop resting my eyes and lift myself up to sitting. The voice is my brother.

"I don't hear anything," I say. "I don't see anything. I don't have it. That's obvious."

"Okay," Lyle says. "That's fine. But there's magic all over. So, fine, maybe you won't get any with skill. There's still luck."

"Luck?" The word used to be mine, used to be my name, but it isn't anymore, it can't possibly be.

"Give it a try, Rose," Lyle says. "There's only a little time left. And a little lucky magic is better than nothing, right?"

"It is?"

"Sure," Lyle says, but he doesn't *sound* sure. He sounds nervous, like he knows what happens if I don't capture any magic at all.

I shrug and open one of my very empty jars. I lift it

into the air and fly it around a little. I set it on the ground and wait. I wave my hands all over, trying to direct magic toward my jar's opening. Lyle copies me, waving his hands, and soon the two of us are making little gusts of wind in the otherwise still air. It makes me laugh and the laugh surprises me because how can I laugh when I've messed everything up? Then Lyle's laughing too, but we quiet ourselves as the sun rises and the sky turns pink and the earliest risers are exiting their cabins, trying to catch a few more drops of magic before the feast.

Maybe it's our waving arms or our laughter or just that I've stopped trying, stopped caring, stopped waiting for it.

Maybe it's simple, simple luck, Little Luck, just not the way Dad meant it when he gave me that name.

Maybe it's just that magic is everywhere by TooBlue Lake and it would be impossible not to catch something.

But mostly it's Lyle and his ability to see magic where others might miss it.

"Oh!" he says. "There!" I follow the tip of his finger and there it is. A blink of light. A tiny spot of sun trapped in glass.

I lunge for the top and twist it on as fast as I possibly can. And then I have it. One jar of magic. One little light. One speck of something.

It's not enough. Not even close. But when I hold the

jar up to the rising sun, it's spectacularly beautiful, a gleam of sunlight that has that early-morning glow. A miniature sliver of warmth.

"Thank you," I say, turning to Lyle. But he's already halfway down the hill, heading back to his friends, his magic. Away from me and everything that's gone wrong. Away from my tiny dimple of lucky magic. The Little Luck.

I watch the lake. My dad's in it now, scooping up the last bits of magic before the sun's all the way up and the capturing is over. He does it like it's nothing, like it's the easiest thing he's ever done, like he was meant to do it. Which I guess he was.

And which I guess I was not.

Fifteen

Breakfast is beautiful. Better than they described.
There are picnic tables, dozens and dozens of them, lined
up in the sand, each decorated with flower petals and jars
shimmering with magic. And food. Piles of croissants and
plums, eggs and pancakes, French toast sprinkled with cinnamon, every kind of cheese I can think of.

I watch from up high on my hill while Mom and Dad
take their place at the head of one of the picnic tables. Dad's
nodding and gesturing to a pile of glass jars by his feet.
Mom's looking around, probably for me. Lyle bounds out
of his cabin, followed by a few of his friends, all of them
carrying jars in their hands and on their backs, rolling some

along with their feet. It looks so easy. I hug my one jar of magic close to my chest and look around for more to catch. But we've always been told the magic is gone when the sun rises on January second; that it's always been that way. When I asked Dad why that was, he smiled. "Magic is special," he said. "It's not for just anyone at any time. It means something."

I nodded, thinking at the time that I understood, but now I hate that rule. I'm ready for capturing *today*. Yesterday I was out of sorts from the way Ginger was acting and all the pressure from my father and the mistake with the lake and remembering the night before Lyle's first capturing. Today I could do it. I know I could. I scrunch my toes, then stretch them. I open up one of my empty jars now and swish it through the air. I jump up as high as I can, then bend low and bury the jar into the dirt. It's pointless. There's nothing magical about today. The dirt is dirt. The air is air. I'm Rose Alice Anders, and I'm nothing special either.

Ginger and Maddy make their way to the beach. They hook arms. They walk in perfect sync, then realize they are walking in sync and collapse into giggles. They try to replicate that rhythm, but it's not there when they try for it. It's the sort of harmony that only emerges accidentally, something you can't coax out of nothing, its own sort of magic.

More and more people come out of their cabins, gasp at the breakfast spread, hurry to sit at a table or to a dock with a doughnut or to a patch of grass with a pile of bread and cheese on a paper plate. I stay on the hill. I count jars. It's easy—everyone's showing them off, lifting them to the sky, pointing at a glimmer or glint or speck of something.

There's so much. Hundreds of jars. Maybe even thousands. It sort of seems like we are drowning in magic. It looks so easy, all tucked away behind glass. How could anyone not catch at least a little?

I lift my one jar up again. It looks like a sunbeam is stuck in there, and it's basically nothing, but it's all I have.

"Rose! Rose Alice!" I hear my mother's voice, and she's looking absolutely everywhere, so she'll look here soon enough. I could wait for her, but there's no point—there's nowhere to hide, and eventually I have to leave the hill next to TooBlue Lake and go back home and be this girl, this Anders kid who was supposed to follow in her father's enormous magical footsteps but instead made a fool of herself.

I might as well be that girl now. I am that girl, whether I'm up on the hill or down there eating pancakes.

And I'd rather be eating pancakes.

"Mom!" I call back, as loudly as I can, but it's not loud enough to drift up and over the voices clamoring to tell the tale of how they caught their first and fifth and eleventh and thirtieth jars. "Mom!" I call again, running down the hill. My speed picks up and the hill is steeper than I thought and I'm more tired than I knew, and the hill gets the best of me; my feet lose their way and I tumble. At first it's just a bit of lost footing, but then my feet get all tangled up and my body can't find any sort of balance, and the trip becomes a topple, which becomes a spectacle of me sliding down a hill, hanging on tight to my jar and a few blades of grass I'd hoped would slow me down.

By the time I'm at the bottom of the hill, I am covered in grass stains and humiliation.

"Look who it is," Maddy says.

"Are you okay?" Ginger asks.

Mom rubs her hands together and searches for what to say.

Dad looks out at the lake and pretends I didn't just show up.

"What do you have there, Rose?" Mom asks when I've straightened myself up and smoothed down some hair.

"I caught a little something," I say.

"How much?" Mom asks.

"This," I say, and hold out my jar. "One."

"Oh. Well. That's okay."

"I tried."

"And that's what matters," Mom says, but the words are tight and Dad's silence is much louder than Mom's forced okay-ness.

"It's a good one," Lyle says.

"Oh, I'm sure," Mom says.

"It was a hard one to catch," he says. "Took a lot of work."

"Sounds very tough."

"Probably no one else could have gotten that one there."

"Well. Congratulations." Mom puts an arm around me and squeezes. She looks at the jar. The sunbeam of magic is in there, and it looked sort of spectacular up at the top of the hill, but down here it's nothing; it's not as brilliant as the sunshine in Maddy's jars or the lake water in Dad's. It's not even as shiny as Lyle's silvery magic. Ginger has a jar that's sort of smoky and strange—something like that would have made a much better impression. Even a bit of cloud or feather or flower or sand would be better than this glint of nothing.

"Thank you," I say.

"In a town with no magic," Mom says, "they'd think this was incredible." She sounds a little sad to say it, and I don't know what she means by it. I think of that clock tower we saw in class, how strange it was, to think of it ticking and tocking from something other than magic.

I look at Mom's face, to try to understand what she's telling me. It's a blurry mix of sadness and wonder that I've seen sometimes late at night after she's fought with Dad and she doesn't know I'm watching her sit on the couch alone, hugging a mug of tea with both hands, sticking her nose in the steam.

She has that tea-hugging, steam-smelling look on her face now.

"You can sit with us," Ginger says. She scoots over on the picnic bench she and Maddy have claimed. She's got three pieces of French toast and a scoop of blueberries and a glass of orange juice that almost looks too orange.

Maddy clears her throat like Ginger's said something wrong, and I wonder what they talked about last night. They have matching T-shirts—blue and white stripes—and I know it's not an accident because nothing's really ever an accident. I don't want to be the odd one out, the obvious third wheel in a non-striped, not-blue shirt and bare feet.

"That's okay," I say. "I'm not even hungry."

I'm starving of course, and I've been waiting for this meal for my entire life, but nothing will taste good right now. Especially if I have to watch Ginger and Maddy become magical best friends without me.

"Mom? When are we heading home?" I ask.

The bus ride home is another tradition I've been hearing about since I was a baby. Everyone tells the story of their hardest capture and shares one thing they hope their magic does. Some of the kids make a joke out of it, and some take it very seriously, talking about world peace and curing cancer, as if maybe they got some sort of extra-strength magic and not just garden-variety pass-the-math-test/make-the-roses-grow-faster/make-my-broccoli-taste-like-chocolate-for-one-night magic.

What Magic You Got Your First Year is a story people ask you to tell all the time. People like to talk about where they were when a certain president was elected, or what their wedding was like, or the most embarrassing thing they did when they were a kid. It's a fact about a person, a thing you're never too far away from. Hair color, eye color, profession, how many jars you caught last year, how many jars you caught your first year.

I try to take in that this will be a fact about me forever, and it's too hard to think about, it hurts too much, so I try to think about nothing at all. That doesn't work either, not with the lake lapping and Dad refusing to look at me and Ginger looking at me too closely.

I know one thing for sure. I cannot go on that bus.

"I'm done with breakfast now," I say. "I think we should head home."

Mom has a piece of sourdough bread with strawberry-apple jam in one hand and a slice of bacon in the other. "I see," she says.

"I'm done too," Lyle says. He shoves the remainder of a maple scone into his mouth.

"You are," Mom says.

"We should really get going," I say. "Dad? I'm ready to go home now." I need him to look at me. I need to know I'm still here, even if I only have this one jar, even if I'm not exactly who he thought I would be.

His face is hard. But it finally turns my way. "You go," he says. "I'll catch up."

"Catch up?" Mom asks. None of what is happening was supposed to happen, and Mom can't seem to keep up with all the changes in the script.

"*I'll catch up,*" Dad says again, gruffer this time. He looks back at TooBlue Lake. It really is too blue. Bluer than any lake needs to be.

Mom puts down the toast. Eats the bacon. Gathers up her jars and puts the ones she can fit in her backpack. There's not room for all of them, and Dad's not moving to help her carry them to the car the way he usually would. Lyle doesn't have any free arms either.

"Rose?" Mom says, trying to whisper, but it's pointless because everyone could hear a cricket chirp right now, that's how quiet it is. "Can you help me?"

"Sure," I say, and I pack the rest of my mom's jars into my empty backpack. I try not to look at them as I put them away, but they're beautiful, a blue glow in one, something purple and shiny in another, ones with dirt and grass and one that looks like it's vibrating.

I wish they were mine.

Sixteen

A Story I'm Thinking About As We Drive Away, About Why Magic Matters and What Is So Beautiful About It and How It Can Change Everything, If You Have It, Which I Don't

Four years ago, Lyle and I asked Dad why magic mattered.

"Is that a real question?" Dad asked. He grinned. When he liked one of our questions, he'd answer with a story better than anything we'd ever find in books.

"It's a real question," I said with a grin just like Dad's. When things were like this with Dad, it felt so good I wanted to hang on to it forever. We were sitting on the couch, Lyle reading, Dad lining up jars on the coffee table, me watching the two of them do what they liked best, and wondering how it would feel when I could line up my own jars next to Dad's, when I finally turned into the person he promised I would be.

"Why does magic matter . . ." Dad said, like he'd never considered it. But it didn't take him long to decide on the right story for the question. "Look there," he said, pointing at a photograph above the fireplace. "What do you see?"

"A rainbow," I said.

"That's been there forever," Lyle said. "Is it magical?"

"Wait," Dad said. He always sounded a little tenser, a little less patient when Lyle was the one asking questions. "Just look at it. Have you ever really looked at it?"

We hadn't. The rainbow over the fireplace was like everything else in our home that we saw but didn't really *see*. It was like the color of the walls in the bathroom or the knobs on the closet doors. A fact of the place, not a feature. But we looked now. The rainbow was extra bright. It looked a little fake, on top of the cloudiness of the sky. It was exactly what a rainbow was meant to be—the colors in the right order, the whole thing arching perfectly, what I would draw if someone instructed me to draw a rainbow.

"What do you think?" Dad said. He crossed his arms over his chest and leaned back, looking at it himself.

"It's a rainbow," Lyle said.

111

"It's beautiful," I said.

"It's my first magic," Dad said. "Well, my first magic that really worked."

I don't know about Lyle, but I looked at the photograph with new eyes. I wanted to understand everything about how it happened and what he did to make it appear and what it meant.

I hummed out a "wow" and Lyle shifted in his seat and Dad let it land.

"I promised my parents I'd save my magic for something important," he said at last. "We'd talked about what to use magic for. Curing illnesses. Passing exams. Fixing the hole in the roof of our little house. I wanted to be useful. I wanted to do it right."

"I want to do it right," I said.

Lyle sighed. He didn't like talking about magic. Not his own. Not Dad's. And especially not mine. Sometimes I wondered if Lyle wished he could be in a different family, where he could capture his jars on New Year's Day and use them for whatever and not think too much about any of it.

Sometimes—less often, and only when I was almost asleep—I wondered if I'd like that too.

"A day or two after I captured my first jars of magic, I walked into the kitchen and my mother was crying. I'd never seen her cry before. You never met her, but she

112

wasn't— Some people cry. She wasn't one of those people. But there she was, crying anyway. Her shoulders shaking. Nose running. The whole thing. Awful."

"Why?" I asked.

"Don't know," Dad said. He shrugged, like the why wasn't important to the story. Dad's stories were often this way. The things I wanted to know he didn't have answers for; the parts of them that seemed important to me were silly details to him. "I don't know what the crying was about, but it was so hard to watch and I couldn't stand it. I had to do something to make it stop. And I had all this new magic, so I went right for my jars. I thought I'd make the most beautiful thing I could think of."

"A rainbow," I said.

Lyle was quiet. He twirled a tassel of a throw blanket around his finger.

"Now, what I didn't know is that weather is almost impossible to do well. It's hard to do at all. Some people will never get that advanced," Dad said. We knew this already. Weather was one of the bigger magics. Not impossible, not incredibly rare. But difficult to do well, requiring some artistry. "I didn't know it would be hard, I just knew my mother would like to look out her window and see something besides the gray sky. So I set out to work. And it took all day and all night and most of my magic. I kept opening jars that had nothing to do with weather and making all kinds of silly mistakes. I was unpracticed. I magicked up some crayons. I made a rainbow-colored cake. I turned my hair rainbow colored. But finally, finally I did it. And once it was there in the sky, it was perfect. More brilliant than anything anyone had ever seen. My mother stopped crying. Whatever was making her sad stopped mattering as soon as that rainbow reached the sky."

I looked at the photograph again. It was a very pretty rainbow. But I couldn't imagine it fixing something that was making his mother cry. Maybe I had to have seen it in person to understand. Maybe I had to make one myself.

"She must have been so proud of you," Lyle said. I was surprised he was the one to say it. And he looked a little sad, letting the words come out, like it was something he'd never have for himself.

Dad shrugged. "She grounded me for a month. I wasn't supposed to use magic for things like that, she said." He looked at the rainbow hard. "But it wasn't a mistake. I didn't apologize. It worked. It changed things. That's what magic's for."

I nodded. Lyle nodded too. I liked the story. And I also didn't understand it, exactly. But it was an important story, and if I wanted to be Little Luck, if I wanted to be the next-most-magical person in all of Belling Bright and maybe also the world, I'd have to understand it someday.

And that meant I'd have to make a rainbow.

I looked at Lyle. We were good at speaking without speaking. And even though it meant something different to him, even though the story hit him in other places, made him feel other things, I knew he wanted to make a rainbow too. And that someday we'd do it together.

Seventeen

No one's on the road. They're all on the beach.

The roads away from TooBlue Lake are curvy, and on the bus I didn't notice it so much, but in our family car, stuffed with magic that isn't mine, sitting in the back next to Dad's red parka that he insists would only encumber his magic capturing, I'm woozy. It's quiet. Lyle scans the radio, looking for something with too many guitars and lyrics I won't be able to understand. Mom makes a little sighing noise at every turn, and I know she has something to say—probably a lot of somethings—but she isn't saying anything at all.

We drive like that for a while until we reach the Belling Bright Woods with its tall trees and magical growth. Lyle says he has to use a bathroom and Mom says she needs a coffee, and I'd like to ask for breakfast but am too embarrassed to say anything at all. Besides, I don't deserve breakfast. I don't deserve lunch or dinner either.

Mom stops the car at a rest stop. It's a small brick building in a field of dandelions and long grasses. There's a bench and a hammock out front. I must have seen it before—we are right outside Belling Bright, not very far from our own home—but it's not the kind of place I'd ever remember.

"Who will be here?" Lyle asks. "Isn't everyone at the lake?"

"Not everyone," Mom says.

"Who wouldn't be at the lake?" Lyle asks.

Everything shuts down from New Year's Day morning until January 3—the library, the post office, the grocery store in the center of our little town, even the twenty-four-hour diner by our house closes, hanging a sign in the window that proclaims: *We will reopen soon—more magical than ever!*

"Just some people," Mom says. "People who don't— there's a few people without much—people who aren't interested in magic."

My heart stops. Or I stop feeling it for a moment. We have never heard those words in that order. We've never even thought them. Magic is magic. It's the thing that helps you do other things. It's not some preference, like how I'm not really into soda even though everyone seems to love it, or Lyle isn't into camping even though Dad says he loved camping when he was Lyle's age.

"Not Meant for Magic," Mom whispers, like she almost doesn't want us to hear her, but then she smiles a tiny bit, like maybe she's happy we have. The smile vanishes before I'm even sure I've seen it. Maybe it was never there at all.

There are lights on in the rest stop, and the smell of something cinnamony baking, and, if I look closely, shadows moving around behind the closed floral curtains. But we haven't left the car.

"Not Meant for Magic," I repeat. They're the first words I've spoken since we left the lake, and they feel too right in my mouth. They feel like they belong to me.

"I've been up all night," Mom says. "This isn't the kind of conversation we can have on no sleep. And without your father. And in a parking lot." She rubs her forehead. "I just wanted a coffee. I didn't mean to open a whole— We agreed to wait to— We should have kept driving."

"Well, we're here now," Lyle says. He rolls down his window and raises his head up and out. He sniffs the air like maybe there's some scent that will explain it all.

I just keep looking and looking and looking.

"We can get back on the road," Mom says. "It's just another mile. I'll brew some coffee at home. Make us a couple sandwiches. We can sit on the porch. We can read or play cards. Dad will be home, you know, sometime. There's no reason to be here." She turns the key, restarts the car.

"I want to know what *Not Meant for Magic* means," I say. My heart twirls again from the words.

"Rose," Mom says. But my name isn't an answer or an explanation. It's just my name, all bare and lonely by itself.

"Am *I* Not Meant for Magic?"

"Rose," Mom says again.

I watch Lyle pull his head back into the car. He stares at his hands. Even being the brother of someone Not Meant for Magic is probably a bad thing. And Mom isn't saying no. She isn't saying anything.

"I caught a little," I say, but even I don't believe that means anything good. "Maybe I'm just meant for a little magic. Magic knows, right? Magic decides who you are and who you're meant to be?" I'm saying it to make myself feel better, but it makes me feel worse.

My one jar is so slight, so dim; if that's all magic thinks I deserve, something must be very, very wrong with me.

"I wish your dad were here," Mom says.

"He's not," Lyle says.

Mom nods. And nods. And nods. And finally speaks. "Some people try to capture magic and just—it doesn't come naturally. And they decide—some of them—to forget about it. To live their lives without."

The quiet is almost violent. It prickles my skin.

"They decide?" I ask. "Or magic does?" Dad's always made it sound like magic decides everything, like he is who he is because magic said it was so.

Mom pauses. She doesn't like to answer things like that.

There's a knock on Mom's window, and it makes us all jump in our seats. Mom gasps. Lyle chokes on nothing. I just look. I am more alert now than I was the entire night at TooBlue Lake. There's a girl my age attached to the knock and she's got a round face and straw-colored hair and tiny hands and a big red flannel shirt like the kind Dad wears on weekends and Mom wears to bed sometimes and I would never wear because none of the girls at school ever wear flannel.

I have a big collection of fuzzy sweaters and floral T-shirts and stripy dresses and black and gray and blue leggings and things that sparkle a little but not too much. And of course, Dad's sweaters and scarves, a dozen of each, and they go with everything, even dresses that I hate but that I wear when Mom or Ginger asks me to.

"Hi!" the girl in the flannel shirt says. "Can we help you?"

I can see Mom's eyes in the rearview mirror and they are enormous. Lyle is looking at me like I know how to talk to other twelve-year-old girls, even ones who aren't meant for magic.

Maybe especially ones who aren't meant for magic.

"We need coffee," I say. "Or my mom does. And a bathroom. My brother needs that. And—something to eat? Maybe?"

"I'm Zelda," the girl says.

"Okay," I say.

"And you are?"

"Rose," I say. "Rose Alice Anders." People know my name. Even people on the edge of town who I've never seen before have heard about my dad and his lucky daughter.

It's true, because Zelda's eyes get as wide as Mom's. She looks from me to Mom to Lyle, and all the way back around again. "You're—really? I thought—my dad always said you wouldn't ever come here."

Mom clears her throat. Shakes her head. Clears her throat again. Shakes her head even more firmly. Zelda looks confused and I feel confused and Lyle finally speaks up.

"You know about Rose," he says. "Of course you do." Maybe yesterday he would have been annoyed or envious or just bored with the way people talk about me and my dad, but today he remembers that everything has changed and he hangs his head.

Zelda laughs. It's a big laugh; the only other person I know with a laugh like that is my dad, and I hadn't really wanted to think about him at all right now, but Wendell Anders is everywhere, impossible to avoid, even at a random

121

rest stop a mile outside of town.

"Well, of course we know about Rose!" Zelda says. She beams.

"Everyone does, don't they?" Mom says. Her voice is shaky and she's talking fast like she does when she's nervous. "Rose is famous. Like her dad. Even perfect strangers have heard of her. Which is—I'm sure it's been a lot of pressure. And maybe that's why—or maybe it will be nice for her to have a break from all the attention—but regardless, yes, even a stranger we've never met before knows our family, how funny, right?"

It isn't funny, and my mom isn't being herself. She sounds the way I feel inside. All hectic and worried and speeding through a million new understandings of the way things are going to be now.

"Right," Zelda says, about a hundred times slower than Mom. "Even strangers like me know Rose Alice Anders." I wait for her big booming laugh, but it's gone, like it was never here at all. She puts her hands in her jeans pockets and keeps staring at Mom.

There's a moment of silence, and even though this girl's a stranger, I don't want her to know how weird we all are right now, so I speak up and try to get us back on track. "So, um, can we get some food and coffee and stuff?" I ask.

"The sign says open," Zelda says with a shrug. She points at the sign above the rest stop. It's the same floral pattern as the curtains with shiny gold lettering on top: *Open 24 Hours. Every Day. Really. Every Single One of Them.*

"Well, yes, look at that, that's right." Mom's voice is chirpy, like she swallowed a bird, and Lyle looks relieved at being able to use a bathroom after all this awkwardness.

"Well, if you're open, then I guess we're coming in," I say, looking at my mom and Lyle and my mom again. I know I've made everything in our life confusing and wrong and mixed-up, but there shouldn't be anything so confusing about picking up a doughnut, even if it's from a person who isn't meant for magic, in a town where I thought everyone was meant for at least a little.

Zelda smiles. "Well, great," she says. "Visitors. The Anders family. On January second. Who would have thought?"

Eighteen

The rest stop is more like a home, and the people there are, I'm pretty sure, a family. Zelda's family. There's a girl Lyle's age who looks just like Zelda except her straw-colored hair is in a short pixie cut and her flannel shirt is blue and made for someone much bigger than her. There's a tall man and a short woman and everyone's got a mug in one hand and a pastry in the other, and a sleepy look on their face like the day just began. It confuses me for a second, because my yesterday never really ended, so it could be six in the morning or three in the afternoon and it would probably feel just as right. Or just as wrong.

"Oh!" Zelda's maybe-mom says. She almost drops her pastry. "Oh."

"We have some strangers visiting, Mom," Zelda says very fast, like she doesn't want her mom to have a chance to say anything else. "They—need coffee and a snack."

"A snack," her mom says. She nods slowly.

"And the restroom. Do we have any scones left?" Zelda says.

"We sure do," Zelda's mom says. She has a lazy smile, as if part of the point of smiling is the journey to get there and not the smile itself.

She points Lyle to the bathroom and stares at my mother, who won't meet her gaze. The morning is strange here, but it was strange out there too, so it's hard to say why anyone's acting the way they're acting.

It smells like butter and cinnamon inside. There's a kitchen table and a bunch of mismatched chairs. There's a little fireplace that's got a fire almost too big for it burning inside. There's a big brown couch that looks like it's seen a lot of pillow fights and its cushions have built about a hundred forts. The girl I assume is Zelda's older sister keeps laughing at the book she's reading, and the man who is maybe their dad peers over her shoulder every time she giggles, like he can't stand to see a joke pass him by.

He looks up at us and tilts his head. "The Anders family," he says. It's not unusual for people to know us without us knowing them, so I know to smile and not act too snotty about it.

"It's us," I say.

"It sure is," Zelda's maybe-dad says, before turning back to the other girl's funny book. I get the sudden urge to make him laugh the way that book is making his daughter laugh. He seems calm and steady and easy to please, and I just want to make someone happy today.

But I can't think of anything to say that's funny or cute or charming, so I just take a step closer to my mom and lean my head against her shoulder, where I feel safest.

Zelda's mom ducks behind a pastry counter that looks out of place in what otherwise seems like a living room or dining room or kitchen or all three rolled into one. She emerges with three of the biggest scones I've ever seen, absolutely drenched in a yellowish icing. "A scone without icing is like—" She started the sentence like she knew where it was going, but she pauses, clearly having no idea where it's meant to end up. "Well," she says. "I'd say it's like a New Year's Day without magic, but that's not so bad anyway. I guess it's more like—" She pauses again. She doesn't seem worried by the pause. She looks at the fire, at the ceiling, at me. "Like a winter without snow. It happens from time to time, but no one really likes it. And everyone's thinking the same thing—*Is this really winter at all?*" She hands me and Mom our scones, and I can't help but smile. It's true. It doesn't feel like winter's begun until we gather around the window and watch the first snow, which is often the only

126

snow in this part of the country, until Dad dares us to go outside barefoot in it, until Mom says that's too dangerous, until Lyle sticks his head out the window, his tongue out of his mouth, and says snow tastes like ketchup, like anchovies, like cake.

Mom turns the scone over and over in her hands like she's never seen such a pastry, but I have a feeling it's the person who gave it to her that she's really trying to figure out.

"Who doesn't love the snow?" Mom says, in this sad sort of voice, and Zelda's mom nods back with equal sadness, and so I try to look sad too, or at the very least wistful. But it's hard, because the scone smells incredible.

I take a bite. It's delicious and strange. I'd thought the icing would be lemon, but it's not.

"Pineapple?" I say, the strong taste taking over my mouth.

"I should have warned you," Zelda's mom says.

"No, it's awesome," I say. "I like pineapple. Mom, you'll love it."

Mom blushes. "We ate a lot at the feast," she says. She looks at Zelda's mom. "We already ate," she repeats herself, like she didn't hear her the first time.

"At the feast," Zelda's mom says.

"Yes."

"And now you're here."

"Yes."

Zelda's mom steps away from the table and to my mother's side. She puts a hand on her shoulder, and Mom clears her throat. "Are you okay?" Zelda's mom asks.

Mom looks at me, at Lyle emerging from the bathroom, at the scone in her hand and her car out front. "Yes, yes, of course," she says. It's not convincing. "I'm sorry, I should have properly introduced myself. I'm Melissa Alice Anders, and this my daughter, Rose. My son, Lyle. We're— It's been— We aren't usually— Thank you for the scones."

Zelda's probably-dad laughs. It's a big laugh. "We know who you are," he says. "We know you."

Mom shakes her head. She's always been embarrassed by Dad's fame. Zelda's mom puts a hand on Zelda's dad's arm to quiet him.

I wait for Zelda's family to introduce themselves, but they don't. Everyone's standing around with these strange looks on their faces, each of them looking like they want to say something, then deciding not to.

"We're glad you're here," Zelda's mom says.

My mother nods. I can't place the look on her face. It's sad but confused but happy but scared.

"I'm Elizabeth," Zelda's mom says. "You've met my daughter Zelda. This is our oldest, Lucy. And their dad. Bennett."

"Bennett," my mother repeats.

He nods.

Lyle and I try to decide how to stand, what to do with our hands. I want to unlock what is strange about this moment, about this place and these people and also about my mother, but the answer, I'm pretty sure, is the answer to everything today. My failure is making everything all wrong, is opening up moments like this one that were never meant to be opened.

"So you don't, um, go to TooBlue Lake?" I ask. My mom keeps not speaking but also not leaving, so I have to say something in the spaces that remain, and that's the only thing I can think of.

"We're Not Meant for Magic," Elizabeth says. She says it very easily, like it's fine, like it's as simple as painting your door pink instead of black or taking a vacation somewhere no one else has gone.

"We need to go home," Mom says.

I don't say anything.

Zelda looks at me. I wonder if being Not Meant for Magic means you can tell when someone else isn't meant for magic. I wonder if she can see it on me, the way she'd be able to tell if I had freckles or a missing tooth or bangs that needed a trim.

"We should really be going," Mom says.

"Don't forget your coffee!" Bennett says.

"Oh yes, right, thank you," Mom says. I've never seen her so nervous. If Dad were here and being himself, he'd make a joke about how many cups of coffee Mom drinks a day.

But Dad's not here.

Mom takes her coffee and reaches for her wallet, but Elizabeth gently shakes her head, and for some reason Mom doesn't argue, she just nods and looks at the floor. I thank them for the scones, but before we reach the door, Zelda grabs my hand. "If you ever want to talk—" she says.

"About what?" I ask.

"Magic," she says. She shakes her head. She smiles. "Or not-magic. Or, you know, anything. About us. Or about nothing. Whatever friends talk about."

I shrink. Whatever she sees in me is magic-less and strange, like her. I don't want to look that way; I want to hide whatever she's catching sight of.

"I have magic," I say.

"Oh?"

"A jar," I say.

"Oh."

"It's enough," I say.

"I didn't say it wasn't," she says. She shrugs. "But it's not a lot."

I want to ask her what she knows about magic anyway, if she's never studied for New Year's Day, if she's never tried to capture any.

Still, she looks at me like she *knows* something. Maybe

not about magic. But about me. And I'm feeling like I don't know too much about either of those things anymore.

"We'll see each other again," she says before letting go of my hand.

"Probably not," I say, but she sounds so sure, her head is so steady, her shoulders so relaxed, that it's easier to believe her than myself.

I pay attention the whole way home. I watch the way the road winds and which trees are where. I make a map in my mind of how to get from here to home and back again. Not because I plan on going back. Not because I want to see Zelda and her family again. Not because I am Not Meant for Magic.

Just because.

Nineteen

A Story About the Other Time
I Went to TooBlue Lake, a Secret
Almost No One Knows

Dad took us to TooBlue Lake, once.

Not me and Lyle and Mom. He said Mom and Lyle wouldn't understand.

He took me and Ginger.

"Is this allowed?" Ginger asked a dozen times on the car ride there. She whispered it to me at first, then turned her attention to Dad, asking him over and over and over what the rules were.

"There are no rules," Dad said. I didn't think this was exactly true. Our teachers spoke of magic-capturing rules, and there were signs every few miles on the road to TooBlue Lake reminding us of some of them: *You can't capture magic any time but New Year's Day. You can't capture magic until you turn twelve. You can't live here. You can't swim here. You can't run fast here. You can't take photographs. You shouldn't really be here at all, probably, and will have to answer a bunch of questions if anyone finds you.*

Dad shrugged them all off.

"Those are suggestions," Dad said. "There's no law. It's a public space. Plus, I'm Wendell Anders. This is my lake, isn't it?" He smiled because it was a joke, but I think it felt true to him too. It felt true to me. My father was Wendell Anders, the most magical person in all of Belling Bright and maybe the world, and if it was anyone's lake, maybe it was a little bit his.

My heart surged with the thought. Because I was like my father, and that meant TooBlue Lake was a little bit mine, too.

When we finally got to the beach, Ginger was a panicked mess and I was kind of excited. We were wearing our bathing suits under our clothes and it was a hot July day. If we'd stayed home Mom would have shown us how to make Popsicles and we could've set up the sprinkler in the front yard and run back and forth and back and forth in our new matching bathing suits.

Instead, we were here, and the lake was bluer than I'd ever seen, and Dad practically ran for the water, throwing his shirt off on his way, letting it fly out behind him, landing wherever, it didn't matter, since we were the only people here anyway.

"We can't," Ginger said. She was leaning against the car like it was an anchor.

"If my dad says it's okay, then it's okay," I said. "Trust me."

"I don't want to," Ginger said.

"Well, I want to," I said. I took off my shorts and the blue tank top I always wore on the hottest days. I ran all the way to the water, feeling like a zebra in my black-and-white-striped bathing suit. And I dove in. Even though it said not to. Even though I was pretty sure it was against the rules. Even though Ginger was keeping one finger on Dad's car and peering at me nervously with the rest of her body.

It felt good, the water. Cold. Lake water is always colder than you think it's going to be.

"Look at you! My little lucky mermaid!" Dad called from farther out in the lake than I thought I could swim.

"No one's here!" I said. All the lakes I'd ever been to had been filled with families, kids littler than me running around, building sandcastles, older kids playing volleyball, parents putting sunblock on every limb they could get their hands on. TooBlue Lake was empty.

"They're all afraid," Dad said. "But you don't get magic by being scared."

I waded farther in.

"So Ginger won't get any magic?"

Dad looked over my shoulder to Ginger. She had shuffled a little bit farther away from the car and was pulling at her shirt like she might almost be ready to take it off.

"She might be okay," Dad said with a smile. "Ginger! Over here! You've got this!"

"I'm not a very good swimmer," she called back.

"All the more reason to practice!" Dad said.

"I thought you didn't believe in practice," Ginger said. She was starting to smile. Once Ginger started to smile, she didn't stop, so I knew that in no time at all she'd be splashing around in the lake. Ginger took time to get happy, but once she was there it was big and full and relentless.

"We're practicing swimming, not magic capturing," Dad said. "I believe in practicing swimming."

She took a few more steps away from the car. Her toes were on the sand, her heels still on the parking lot pavement. "Shouldn't we practice swimming at a normal lake? One we're allowed to be at?"

"Look at this place!" Dad said. "You won't be able to look at it when the time comes, not like this. And it's worth seeing."

Ginger looked. I looked. It was really nice, but I don't think I saw what Dad saw. The most interesting thing about TooBlue Lake was how empty it was. The blue was deep and real, but the rest of it was like every other lake. Still water. Mountains like shadows hovering over it. Trees all over the place, different sizes and shapes and degrees of green. Sand that wasn't extra soft and a sky that was gray and air that was muggy. It smelled like summer—kind of sweaty and yellow. The way sunscreen smells when it's baked on your skin for an hour to two.

Finally, Ginger walked over to the lake. She didn't step in. She motioned me over to her.

"I'm scared," she said.

"Why? My dad's here. Everything's fine." Dad was doing somersaults in the water. He looked like a little kid, but also like my dad still.

"My dad said to follow the rules," Ginger said.

Ginger's dad had died not very long before that day, and I could still hear his voice in my head when she said things like that. Her dad hadn't been much like my dad. He was shorter, for one, and quieter. He caught magic every year, a normal amount. Twenty jars, maybe twenty-two. Enough. And the magic inside was fine. Useful. Fixing a car or the air conditioner. Making the dog behave. Once he was even able to put more stars in the sky. I loved that night. Dad was jealous, I think, of that jar of magic. Hundreds of new points of light crowded the night.

Ginger was so proud.

My dad said it wasn't as powerful a magic as magic that could make the moon grow or the seasons change, and I nodded in agreement but wondered in my own head why that even mattered.

Couldn't we just enjoy the stars?

Ginger's dad went to work in a suit and always wore his shoes outside. He played piano in the evenings and didn't smile much, but he didn't not-smile either. When he died, he gave Ginger his college ring and she wore it, now, around her neck. She played with it when she wasn't sure what to do. I wondered how often she thought about that extra-starry night, and if she hoped to capture something similar one day, to remember him by.

I wanted to ask her, but I didn't want her to get that sad look she got when I talked about her dad. So I said nothing, wondering all the while if I should have been saying something.

Dad got out of the water. He always knew what to do and what to say. He bent down so he was face-to-face with Ginger. "Your dad was a great man," he said, loud enough for me to hear, but quiet enough for it to feel like hers alone. "A *great* man. And you should honor the things he told you. But following the rules isn't the way to get magic. And I know your dad was counting on you to get magic for the family. Now that he's gone."

"We follow rules," I said. It wasn't the point, but I didn't like thinking of us as rule breakers and Ginger and her father and her family as perfect rule followers.

"We bend them," Dad said. "We play with them." He splashed Ginger. She gasped from the shock of cold. Even on the hottest day of the year, the lake was icy.

Ginger followed every rule. She had never turned in one sheet of homework late. She ironed all her shirts. She never stayed on the swings for longer than ten minutes even if no one was waiting for them. She wouldn't like Dad telling her to break the rules. She would want to do whatever her dad had told her to do. And maybe she *should* do whatever he said, because he was able to capture that one extra-magical jar of starry magic.

But I didn't say that.

Sometimes, around my dad, I forgot to say the things I wanted to say.

And I didn't need to say anything. Because what Dad had said and done made her pause, but then it made her smile. She swung her arms back. She pushed a giant wave of water forward, getting me and my dad both soaked.

We stayed in the water for hours, for so long that the temperature of the air began to feel strange, the temperature of the water normal. We stayed in there so long that I forgot about magic and New Year's Day and Lyle back home on the couch and how it sometimes felt like Mom and Dad were never in the same place at the same time, how we hadn't had family dinner since Thanksgiving and even that had been quiet in the wrong moments and louder in the wronger moments.

We stayed in the water so long I thought I might not need magic anymore. I might just need a weekly soak in TooBlue Lake, the light in Ginger's eyes, the sound of Dad's limbs splish-splashing in the water.

When the sun was setting we ate cheese and crackers and fruit on the beach.

"I thought a picnic might be nice," Dad said.

"Did Mom pack this?" I asked. I had never known Dad to think of things like the necessity of food. It was Mom who brought tissues and snacks and at least three books and a change of clothes everywhere we went.

"I can put together a picnic!" Dad said. There was no picnic blanket to sit on, and no utensils or plates either. So I believed him that he did it himself. We tore chunks of cheddar from a big block of it and let berry juice run all over our fingers. We didn't complain about sand getting in our mouths, in our hair, in our bathing suits.

None of that mattered.

"This is the best day of my whole life," Ginger said when we were down to a small mound of Havarti, three crackers, and a banana.

"The best day of your life will be New Year's Day," Dad said.

"That will be the best day of *Rose's* life, not mine," Ginger said. "I won't do anything special."

"Sure you will," I said. "Maybe you'll get some of that starry magic that your dad caught."

Ginger beamed. I did too; I was so happy to have finally said the right thing about her dad, to have made her smile like that.

My dad didn't smile and I tried not to notice it. I even leaned in a little, hoping to block Ginger's view of his not-smiling face.

"When you get a hundred jars of magic, will you still be my friend?" Ginger asked.

"Of course," I said.

"A thousand?"

"Of course!"

"A *million*?"

"No. When I have a million jars I am going to magic myself to Mars and become queen of the planet."

Ginger broke into giggles. "That's fair," she said.

"But you can visit," I said.

"I've always wanted to travel," Ginger said.

"You two," Dad said. He ate the last bit of cheese and broke into the banana too. "You're lucky to have each other."

He looked a little sad, like he wanted a best friend as great as Ginger. I felt a little sad too, because sometimes being so happy made me feel sad that something might change all the happiness.

And I was right. Something did.

We never came back to TooBlue Lake again, but it was a secret that pulsed between the three of us, a thing we'd done that no one else had done. The closest I ever got to feeling magic.

Twenty

When Dad finally comes home from TooBlue Lake, it's late.

Later than late, it's at least midnight and it's been hours upon hours since any of us have said a word. We haven't talked about Zelda or those who aren't meant for magic or the ways I let everyone down or our missing father. Lyle and I are asleep on the floor of the living room, where we've made a fort of pillows like we used to do when we were little.

The sound of Dad coming in the door wakes us up. He slams it behind him, like he doesn't care how late it is. Lyle's hand reaches for mine in the dark, under a pillow.

"It's okay," Lyle says, but I don't believe him.

"He's still mad," I whisper back.

"Maybe it was an accident," he says. "The door's kind of heavy." But it isn't, of course. The door isn't heavy and the day isn't okay and Lyle can't protect me from what it is to be a girl with only one jar of magic.

"Family meeting!" Dad's voice is louder than the door slam.

We know this voice. I feel Lyle shrink away from it. I feel myself start to wilt.

I peek out at Dad. His face is red. His fists are clenched. He is so stiff he could be made of metal.

Mom scurries into the room. "It's late, honey," she says. "We've all had a long day."

"I've had a long day," Dad says. "What have you been doing that's so tough?"

"I think you need rest," Mom says.

"Lyle! Rose! Come down here!" Dad's voice is even louder now. I don't know how to make myself any smaller, but I try.

"We're here," Lyle says. He stands up, letting go of my hand. I've never thought of my big brother as brave, but he is in this moment. I'd keep hiding forever, if it were up to me.

"Rose?" Dad says. "Are you there?"

"Mm-hm." I stay in the pillow fort. I don't get up. I'm not brave like Lyle. I'm not magical like my dad or smart like my mom. I'm not much of anything, it turns out. The

143

pillows are comfortable, the floor feels nice and sturdy underneath me, and I think I could live here, at least until next New Year's Day, when I could try again to be the person I'm supposed to be.

"Is this what you do now? Hide when things are hard?" Dad asks. I am filled with the missing of the father who was here two nights ago, wrapping me in his sweater, telling me how special I was.

"I'm sorry," I squeak.

"What is that supposed to mean?" Dad asks.

"That's it," I say. "'I'm sorry' means I'm sorry."

"Stand up, Rose," Dad says.

"You don't have to, honey," Mom says. "It's late. You're resting. That's okay."

"Stand *up*, Rose," Dad says again, as if Mom's not there at all, as if it's just me and him and no one else in the whole wide world. I have my dad's nose and freckled arms and tough feet and big eyes. If I tried, I bet I'd have his loud voice. I have never so badly wished to take after my mother. If I looked like her and Lyle, maybe no one would have expected much from me. If I hadn't been born the day I was born, maybe one jar of magic would be okay. I wish myself into a hundred other bodies and lives and moments in time, but I'm still right here.

So I stand up. And as I stand something happens to Dad's body. It goes from metal to skin, from tense and

144

upright to something soft and drooping. I watch it happen, and I have to know that I did it.

I thought angry was the worst thing my dad could be. But this is worse.

"What happened?" he asks.

I thought he was here to lecture me about what happened, not ask me for my opinion on it.

"I don't know," I say.

"Did you put on shoes?" he asks.

"No."

"Did you go to the top of the hill?"

"Not at first."

"Were you relaxed?"

"I don't know."

"Were you distracted?"

"I don't know."

"Did you try?"

My throat catches. I can't believe he would even ask. "So hard," I say. "I tried so hard."

Dad nods. I think he believes me. Or at least he wants to.

"Something happened," he says.

"I messed up," I say.

Dad nods. Then shakes his head. Then nods again. "Let me see the jar," he says.

I scurry over to my backpack in the front hall and bring him my jar. It's cloudier than I remember, and the jar barely hums. The magic is weak. I know enough about magic to be sure of that. I know everything about magic, except, I guess, how to actually capture any.

"It's not nothing," Dad says. "There's magic in there."

"Yes," I whisper. I almost tell him that Lyle had to help me get it. I almost tell him about Zelda and the people who are Not Meant for Magic and how when I heard those words they buzzed through me like they belonged to me. But I don't say that because I don't want Dad to yell and I definitely don't want Dad to cry and maybe we can all somehow believe together that one jar of magic is enough.

"It's not nothing," Dad says again, but this time he's saying it to Mom, and Mom is nodding and wiping away a tear.

"It's late," Mom says when we've all nodded and nodded about the not-nothingness of my sad little jar. "We can figure everything out—"

"Everything's fine," Dad says. "There's magic. It's not what we— But it's not like it's nothing—this is just an adjustment." He's mumbling to himself mostly, and while he mumbles he heads upstairs. He doesn't say goodnight, but that's okay because he doesn't say anything awful either, so maybe I'll be able to sleep okay after all.

I'm going to sleep down here in my pillow fort and Lyle's heading up to his room, but Mom stops us before we both go on our way.

"Don't tell him about today," she says. She tries to sound

causal, but there's no casual way to ask us to lie to Dad. "About the rest stop. About that not-meant-for-magic family. He doesn't need to know about all that."

I nod and Lyle nods, but underneath all that nodding is my heart beating and beating and beating because Mom has never asked us to keep a secret from our father. We don't believe in secrets in the Anders family, that's what Dad's always said, so it's what I've always thought is true, but maybe it's not true. The same way maybe my specialness isn't true.

And that's a lot of supposed-to-be-true things turning maybe-not-so-true.

Twenty-one

They bring their magic to school. A jar in a backpack, just in case it's needed. The teachers keep a few jars on their desks, like a warning. They switch them out after the New Year, putting pretty new ones front and center.

Ms. Flynn has a new tiny jar that is full to the brim with a watery, speckled magic. I wonder what it does. I'm sure we're all wondering what it does.

"Rose. Good morning. I'm glad you're here," she says when I walk in, alone, behind everyone else, as if she thought maybe I wouldn't be showing up at all.

"Oh," I say, "yeah. I'm here. It's school, right? So I'm here."

"It's school, right?" Maddy, from her desk by the window, repeats my words in a super-high, super-breathy voice that isn't anything like mine. I turn to face her. On her desk are two unnecessarily huge jars, one that looks empty aside from a single blade of grass, another that is filled with purple petals. She sees me seeing them and gives me a smug smile. She's meaner than she was a few days ago.

"Did you bring your jar?" she asks. I wait for Ms. Flynn to tell her to be quiet, but she doesn't.

"No," I say.

"Kept it at home?" Maddy asks. The corners of her mouth keep twitching, like she's excited to be mean to me.

"Yep. I kept it at home. For safekeeping. Since I only have one, you know?"

"Oh, I know," Maddy says. But her mouth corners have stilled. She can't insult me if I've already insulted myself.

"That's a good idea," Ginger says. I look to the corners of her mouth to see if they look like Maddy's. Her lips aren't twitching, though. Her face is quiet, waiting for me to do or say something, but I don't know what I'm supposed to do or say.

Ginger takes her seat. I'd like to move to a corner of the room. A hidden place, maybe tucked behind a curtain or underneath a chair or something. But there's nowhere to hide, so I sit next to Ginger and try not to look at her jars of magic—delicate little things lined up on the right side of her desk, away from me, like she's scared I'm going to steal one or something.

"There's always next year," Ginger says, leaning over to whisper into my ear while Ms. Flynn is turned toward the whiteboard.

"I know that," I snap. "I'm fine."

"I know you thought—" Ginger starts.

"I didn't want more," I spit back. My body stands up even though I didn't tell it to. "I got what I wanted. I don't need— I'm fine. Magic chooses who—magic chose me to get the one most important jar in all of Belling Bright. You'll see." My voice is getting louder than I mean for it to be. So loud that everyone in class can hear me.

Ginger's eyes are wide. She doesn't believe me. I don't believe me either, so I don't blame her.

"Rose. Do you need a minute to compose yourself?" Ms. Flynn asks.

"I'm composed."

"Rose." There's a warning in her voice now. I know the tone—I've heard it directed at kids in my class a bunch of times, but never at me.

I sit back down. I can feel magic buzzing around me. Some of the jars tremble a little. Some hum. Some are still and sparkle quietly. Back home, my jar of magic sits in my closet. I planned to line up all my jars on my windowsill, so everyone walking by could see the best ones. But I can't bear the thought of a single jar just sitting there, looking all lonely and sad and desperate.

Ms. Flynn starts talking to us about the rules of bringing magic to school. I turn to my notebook and start doodling. For months and months I've been trying to draw a picture of myself. I'd been hoping I'd capture a sort of magic that could help me with that. I try to believe what I just told everyone. That the magic I caught is something special, that the magic that found me is bigger and better than anyone else's, that I'm still Rose Alice Anders, and meant for something great.

But I can't believe it. It isn't true.

Ms. Flynn moves on to math, and Ginger passes me a note.

Are we still friends? it says, in Ginger's messy scrawl. I look at her, to see if she means it nicely or meanly or in some other way that I don't yet understand. Usually we pass notes about what we're doing on Saturday and who has more homework and what annoying thing Lyle said and whether Ginger's littlest sister is being cute or impossible these days. Sometimes we pass notes that say *I'm sad* or *I'm tired* or just a face with a straight-mouthed expression that means something like *I want more than to be sitting in this classroom smelling whatever new shampoo Anne is using and watching the clouds move across the sky. I want more than these people and this town and this squeaky, too-hard chair, and I'm going to get it someday, but not today, definitely not today; today I just have to be right here.*

We have never used our note passing to confirm the status of our friendship.

I play with the edges of the paper and turn it around and around in my hands, as if maybe it will make more sense to me upside down. It doesn't.

I don't know what happened, I write back. I mean in our friendship but also at the lake. I mean everything.

I don't even know what we're fighting about, Ginger writes back. She looks the same, but I've never seen the shirt she's wearing before, and I swear she's taller, or maybe just sitting up straighter. I think of making a list of what we are maybe fighting about. *You got the sneakers. You started liking Maddy more than we agreed to like Maddy. You said I don't listen to you. You acted embarrassed by me when I needed a friend. You changed all the rules of our friendship and it made me fail on the most important day of the year and I blame you in all the moments in which I'm not blaming myself.*

But I don't write any of that. It's true, sort of, but it's all sort of not true, too.

I know what you think of a girl who only has one jar of magic, I write back. It's a test. I want her to tell me I'm wrong and she doesn't care and no one cares and no one will notice and nothing will change. If she can tell me all of

152

that—or even some of that—maybe we can find our way back to our friendship. Maybe we can bake cookies together for the bake sale and wear matching outfits to the dance and roll our eyes at Maddy behind her back. Maybe she can sleep over and we can bike ride out to our favorite candy store and bring back bags of chocolates in our bike baskets. Maybe I can stop thinking about Zelda and her little cozy home and the way she looked at me like I might belong there, too.

Ginger writes something down. She scribbles it out and writes something else down. And again and again until there's no more room left on the paper we've been using and she has to switch to a new sheet of paper.

The tearing of that new piece of paper makes Ms. Flynn's head turn back to us, and when she does she catches sight of Ginger scribbling something that is obviously not notes about fractions, and she hovers over her shoulder and taps her foot until Ginger looks up, startled.

"Would you like to share with the class?" Ms. Flynn says. It's what she always says when she catches people—never us!—passing notes in class.

"No, thank you," Ginger says.

"Should I share it with the class?" Ms. Flynn asks.

"No, thank you," Ginger says, a little more forcefully.

But Ms. Flynn doesn't care about Ginger's polite *no thank yous*. Ms. Flynn only cares about fractions and whether we

153

will pass our test on fractions. She opens the note that is only supposed to be for me. The note where maybe Ginger will say something that will make me feel like I belong with her again.

Ms. Flynn clears her throat. "'Not everyone's meant for magic,'" she reads from the piece of paper.

There's a hush in the class. Even Ms. Flynn is quiet, realizing she probably shouldn't have read the words out loud. I blush. I don't know what color I turn. I can't see myself. But it feels like I'm sitting on the sun.

It's only a second before Ms. Flynn clears her throat and starts writing on the whiteboard again, but no one cares about five-eighths anymore. No one cares about anything but the fact that my former best friend thinks I'm not as good as everyone else, not as meant for magic. No one cares about anything but poor Rose Alice Anders, who was supposed to be great, but is an enormous disappointment, even to the people who are supposed to love her the most.

And I can't tell them they're wrong. Because I'm the one who's always reminding them that the magic you get means something about the person you are. I'm the one who taught them all the things Dad taught me—that magic finds the people who deserve it, magic knows what's best, magic is everything.

I could stay and let them look at me like that, I guess, but I've had enough of everyone looking at me, wondering why I am the way I am and why I'm not the way I was sup-posed to be. I've had enough of wondering it about myself. I gather up my stuff, which is mostly just a pencil and a notebook and my dad's scarf that I'm still wearing every day even though he probably wants it back so he can give it to a better kid. I rush out of the classroom and out of the school and onto the empty playground and then out, out, out, onto the sidewalks that lead to other towns and better places, and, if you walk fast and far enough, back to TooBlue Lake.

Twenty-two

I walk through the woods, wondering at who magicked up a bush with sparkly green berries or a circle of tulips lined up beside a twinkle-light-growing patch of dirt. I especially wonder who made the largest trees, the ones that must be centuries old, made by people just discovering magic, perhaps, or people who had grown up deep in it, like me.

Eventually, I get to the edge of town, which isn't close to TooBlue Lake. It is sort of close to Zelda and her family, but it's not like I would ever go there. Still, it's the only place I know over here, so I walk in that direction and imagine a new idea will come before I actually arrive at the place I'm definitely not going to go.

But before I get anywhere at all, I'm stopped by the beeping of a horn and a voice I know well, calling my name.

"Rose. Turn around, Rose. Where do you think you're going, young lady? Rose, I'm talking to you." I don't want to turn around. Not to see his disappointed face again. Not to have to sit in The Way Things Are when only days ago we hung out together in The Way Things Will Soon Be. It hurts too much, to reckon with the distance between the two.

"Rose," he says. "I'm not giving up."

"*We're* not giving up," another voice says.

And that voice makes me turn around. The first voice is my father, and I don't want to see him. But the other voice is Lyle, and we promised each other a lot of things. And one of those things is that we'd never turn away from each other.

And the other thing is that we'd never leave each other alone with Dad if he was mad.

So for two reasons, I turn around.

"You're in school," I say to Lyle, which isn't true because he's right here. "I mean, you're supposed to be in school."

"They called me to the office when you left," Lyle says. "You're supposed to be in school, too."

"They didn't exactly want me there."

"Lyle thought you might have come this way," Dad

says, and the words feel heavy, so I look at him and then at Lyle to see if Lyle told Dad about the rest stop and the Not Meant for Magic family and Mom making us promise to keep it a secret. Dad looks exhausted and frustrated, but not anything more than that, so I think we're still keeping the secret.

I know Lyle's face well. He dips his chin when he's nervous and he closes his eyes a little too long on every blink when he's lying. He frowns when he's scared and he blushes when he's mad. I take a good long look at him. He is nervous and unsure and he just lied about why I might be out this way.

"You're my girl," Dad says. "Headed out to the lake to try again. I should have guessed it myself."

It is the opposite of who I am right now, this idea he has of me. My heart twists a little, thinking about the big space between who he thinks I am and who I am.

It keeps growing and growing.

Or maybe it was always this size, but I was trying to pretend it was not.

"Right," I say. "Yes. I need—I wanted to catch magic somehow now. I wanted to try again. For you."

"You have to try for *you*," Dad says. He reaches through the window and grabs my shoulder. In the front seat, Lyle watches. I have watched Lyle watching Dad my whole life. I was watching Dad too, but for different things.

"Okay," I say.

"Maybe that was the problem. Too focused on other people," Dad says.

I nod. Lyle nods. Dad jerks his head back to tell me to climb in, and I do, and we drive, but I keep hearing that sentence in my head. Then I hear more of his sentences in my head. The things he says that sound so sure and solid. They always have. *Magic knows. Magic gives you what you deserve. You are Little Luck. Magic is the most important thing. Don't try. But also be great. But also you are great, and magic will see it. You are special. You are mine. We are the same.*

He never says *I think* or *maybe* or *probably.*

Wendell Anders is always sure.

But I am Rose Alice Anders. And maybe I've never actually been sure of anything.

"How do you know?" I say, when we are pulling into the lake's parking lot. The wheels hit some ice, but Dad knows how to steer on something slippery, so it barely feels scary for more than a second.

"Know what, Little Luck?" he asks, and I wish I could tell him to stop calling me that, the way I asked my mother to stop calling me Baby Girl a few years ago when it was getting embarrassing.

Little Luck is worse than embarrassing.

159

It feels almost like something I better become, something I have failed at and have one more chance to get right. And that one more chance is right now.

"How do you know how magic works?" I ask. "How do you know all the things you know? We don't learn them exactly that way at school. And some families think—"

"How much magic do those families have?" Dad asks. He parks, his arm working a fraction too forcefully to stop the car. The car jerks just a little.

"We have the most magic," Lyle says, and I know he wants me to stop, but I can't.

"How do you know that of all the people in Belling Bright, you are meant to be the most magical?" I ask. It's a question I didn't know I'd wanted to ask my whole life. A question that Ginger asked once, a few days after her own father died. She had a lot of questions that day. Why my dad's magic couldn't save her dad. Why her dad had to die. Why magic existed, if it couldn't fix anything real. I kept stumbling around the answers, never quite finding one that fit.

"Never mind," Ginger had said at last. "None of it makes sense anyway. Magic isn't the answer to everything."

"Yeah," I'd said, and I'd been wanting to ask Dad about it ever since.

"I know I'm meant to be the most magical because I

am the most magical," Dad says. He looks at me very hard. Then at Lyle, who is looking right back at him.

"But why?" I ask.

"Because I know how to use it," Dad says. He's speaking slowly, but his hands are tight on the wheel and I should have asked this when we were out of the car.

"Not always," I say.

"Rose, let's go look at the lake," Lyle says.

"What does that mean, 'not always'?" Dad asks.

I shake my head. I said it wrong. Or I said it right, but I didn't want to say it at all.

"It didn't mean anything," Lyle says.

"It didn't mean anything," I echo. "I don't even know what I'm saying."

Dad nods. When Dad's angry, it's big. But he takes his time getting there. It's why I got mad at Maddy when she said she heard my dad had a temper. A temper means you are quick to anger. That's not my father at all. That's not him right now. He takes a big breath, like he's resetting the whole day, and by the time he's done exhaling, he's getting out of the car and opening our doors.

"Magic matters," Dad says, like he has a million times before. "And it will find you, if you're ready for it, Rose."

I nod.

"Are you ready?" he asks.

I wasn't, and I'm not, and I also maybe don't want to be. But Lyle is looking cold and nervous and the lake is looking quiet and strange and I want one last gasp of being Little Luck before I have to go back to being the girl with one jar of magic, so I nod again. "I'm ready," I say, and it's a lie. And it has always been a lie.

Twenty-three

The snow crunches under our feet, and Dad hums because even with everything that's gone wrong, TooBlue Lake is still his happy place. Lyle and I walk a few feet behind him, and I can hear how deep Lyle's breaths are. It's his nervous breathing, a rhythm I learned on our rooftop. A sound that I'm so used to, it's a little like my own heartbeat.

"You're going to capture something, right?" he whispers.

"How would I know?" I ask.

"Rose, you have to. You have to show him—"

"You think I didn't try last time?"

"Even one more jar," Lyle says. "Two. And he'll go back to—it will all go back to the way it was."

"I can't," I say. "I don't hear it."

"You have to," he says. "Take your time. Listen."

Dad keeps rushing ahead, unfazed by the emptiness, by the fact that we aren't really supposed to be here. He takes steps like he's done this before, and I guess he has, like the time he came here with me and Ginger.

That didn't seem like the first time either, though.

He takes a jar from his pocket and flies it through the air, making a whooping sound when he catches something. It's so easy for him. He does another, pulling it through the snow. Smiles at what's inside. Two more jars of magic, just like that.

Lyle and I stop. Lyle listens. I pretend to. I was always pretending. I was pretending to be the Little Luck Dad told me I was. Because he made it sound so true. But every time he said that magic knows what it's doing, I knew that maybe it didn't. And I pretended that I didn't have that doubt. Doubt and wondering why so much magic found him, if it really knew everything.

Because my father is big and brave and booming. He is funny and strange and charming. He makes serious people laugh and he makes silly people think and he made me feel like I could be anything I wanted to be.

Except maybe he mostly made me feel like I could only be what he wanted me to be.

My father is a hundred wonderful things.

But he is also a few not-wonderful things.

And didn't magic see those not-wonderful things?

"I've never heard anything," I say now to Lyle. "Not once. I've never heard anything or felt anything. I've never really been so sure about any of it."

"What do you mean?" Lyle asks. Maybe it was hard, having a lucky younger sister. But it will be even harder to have an unlucky one.

"I don't think I'm meant for magic," I say. "Like Zelda. Like her family."

"You're not Zelda and her family," Lyle says. "You're my family. You're ours."

Dad catches another jar of magic. This can't be allowed. We came here for me to catch up, but Dad doesn't need anything else.

"Of course," I say. "I know." I take out a jar, because the look on Lyle's face says I have to try. But when I try to twist off the top a familiar pain zaps my wrist.

"Oh!" I say.

Lyle looks at me holding my wrist, rubbing it with my thumb. "Your wrist's acting up again?"

"It's probably going to snow," I say.

"Come on, you two, hurry up!" Dad says. "There's magic to be caught!"

My fingers are starting to feel like they're going to freeze off, and I don't like how my words have turned to icicles in the air, hanging over us. You never know how long an icicle's going to stay around, and I'm ready for all of it to melt, right now. I'm ready for the seasons to change.

"I can't," I say.

"Her wrist," Lyle says. Dad stops and takes a deep breath before turning back to us. He doesn't like when we give up, but he knows when my wrist is hurting I have trouble thinking about anything else. It's a mysterious, occasional bone-deep pain that can only be cured with a heating pad and the passage of time. It makes it hard to make a sand-wich or to play softball or to draw. It makes it hard to open a jar and swing it through the air, looking for magic.

"Can you try for one jar?" Dad asks. "Let one jar of magic find you?" He looks like a little kid. Like someone's little brother who wants a scoop of ice cream or a trip to the toy store. He doesn't look like Wendell Anders at all.

"Okay," I say. "I can try to let it come to me."

So we try. Lyle and I. We sit in the snow and wait for the magic to find us. Dad runs back and forth across the beach, catching jar after jar, breezy, bright magic, and sooty gray magic and magic that looks like it would burn you if you stuck your hand inside.

Seventeen jars of magic that I'm not sure are even allowed. Each one caught so easily, so wordlessly, that I only know one thing for sure.

He has done this before. He hasn't been following the rules the rest of Belling Bright follows.

When Dad comes back to us, he's sweaty and full-backpacked. His cheeks are ruddy and he's proud.

"What'd you get?" he asks. He looks at our hands. They are empty. The magic didn't come to us. Not to me. Not to Lyle. Not to our open jars. "Nothing?" he asks, his voice a little louder, his neck a little redder.

"I hear it," Lyle says. "I do hear it."

Dad looks at me. But I'm tired and my wrist aches and I am trying to understand why Dad is allowed to catch seventeen extra jars of magic on January 4 and why he seemed so comfortable doing it. I am trying to do too many other things to manage lying as well.

"I've never heard it," I say. "Even the magic on New Year's Day—I needed Lyle for that. I'm not—I'm not Little Luck. I'm not sure I'm even meant for magic."

Dad doesn't say a word. He stomps toward the car, and for a moment I think maybe Lyle and I will stay here, on the shores of TooBlue Lake, where it's cold but probably warmer than the car with my father will be.

We run to catch up with him. To fix it. Because we have to fix it.

"I'm—" I start, thinking I'll apologize and see where that gets me. But he doesn't let me finish.

"You are Rose Alice Anders," Dad says, and I guess in a different voice it might sound like a pep talk, but it comes out as a snarl. "Little Luck. We are the Anders family. And

you will not embarrass me like this. Your mother will not—
I worked hard to be where we are, and I don't want to hear
another word about it. That jar of magic you caught—we
will assume it is the most magical jar of magic in all of Belling Bright. In all of the world. Because that's who you are
meant to be. I won't hear any different."

"But I told you—" I say, even though my brain is telling
me to stop talking immediately. Dad's voice only gets louder
and surer.

"I told *you*!" he says. If we weren't at the deserted lake,
maybe someone would hear, would ask if everything's okay.
They have asked before.

But we are alone and I am alone and my jar of magic
is alone and nothing is right, it only keeps getting more
wrong. "Not another word. You work things out with your
friends. You shape up. You be who you are meant to be.
Which is magical."

I look to Lyle for what to do or say. But he only gets
in the car. In the backseat with me instead of in the front
with Dad. It's the best he can do for me, and I know that.
He hangs his head. I bet he wishes he could do more, but
what's the point of all our wishing? This is today. This is
our father. This is the inside of the car. There's nothing to
be done about any of it.

We don't speak the whole way home. Dad takes on
turns like they're his enemies and we slip and slide over the

ice. I hang on to Lyle's arm and wish as loud as I can in my head for my father to slow down. But Lyle's giving me *shut up* looks, so I stay quiet and Lyle stays quieter, and Dad puts his foot even harder on the gas, and we go even faster, and nothing, not even my own father, is safe anymore.

I look out the window as we go, but I look extra hard when we pass Zelda's family's rest stop. I'm pretty sure I see Zelda and Lucy sitting out front, sticking their tongues out of their mouths, smiling at the taste of snow. In Belling Bright, kids make the snow taste like strawberries or ice cream or Swiss cheese. But Zelda and Lucy know the taste of snow is perfect because it only tastes like cold, like winter, like the promise of a snow day, like the wonder at white covering the earth.

Some things are better without magic, I think.

Maybe even some people.

Twenty-four

The snow is gone by Friday. Some jar of magic has turned the season into spring. I would have liked a few more weeks of sweaters and mittens and hot chocolate. Maybe seasons stay as long as they're meant to stay and we shouldn't mess with them. Maybe magic isn't the only thing that happens for a reason.

Ginger, Maddy, and another girl named Layla all have the same bright pink streaks in their hair. Ginger has a new gray dress that looks like it's made of something soft and special. I want to touch it. Maddy's skin looks shinier. Or rosier. Or something-er. They all get A's on their math homework. I'm pretty sure they even all smell the same, like apples and vanilla, and that they are, somehow, the same height.

"You grew," I say to Ginger after we get our math homework back. I'm not talking to Ginger, but the words come out anyway. I try to say them in my head, but I'm not very good at keeping things in my head. It would have been a good thing to use magic for. Magic to make my mouth slow down, to make me more careful. Maybe if I had that kind of magic, Ginger and I could be ourselves again.

Maybe, with that kind of magic, my family would be okay.

"I never would have used magic to make me taller," I say, because I'm not about to say all the other things.

"I didn't," Ginger says, but I know she's lying because she whispers it, and she always whispers when she's lying. Ginger hates lying, so she does it really quietly.

"Come on," I say.

"You can't control what kind of magic you get in your jars," Ginger says, which isn't exactly her saying she did in fact use magic to grow, but it kind of really *is* her saying that.

"You did your hair too."

It's common for the youngest capturers to get the silliest magic. That's how it works. That's what we're meant for, I guess.

Then I remember I don't even have the silliness, I only have my one jar of practically nothing.

That's all I was meant for, I think. *I deserve less than the silliest, smallest things. I am almost worthless.*

"We always said we'd do our hair," Ginger says. "If we got the right kind of magic."

"Right," I say. "But I didn't do it." I try to make my back as straight as I can, in case Ginger can somehow see all the things I'm thinking. There is magic that helps you know what someone is feeling. It doesn't usually find someone as young as us, but Ginger is looking at me with a strange new look on her face, so who knows.

"Well, yeah. I mean, I figured you can't. Unless you think that's the kind of magic that's in your jar?"

"Yeah. I mean, I just wouldn't."

"So. Right. I have more than one jar. So I can try—"

"You can do anything you want, I guess," I say.

It seems like a hundred years ago that Ginger and I made our list of the top one hundred things to do with our magic. Get matching pink hair was somewhere around number twenty-two. After we magick ourselves to Bermuda and before magically fixing Lyle's bike.

Lots of kids open their jars of magic and find that what they'd hoped would make them taller is actually a magic for growing trees, or that magic they thought was for getting a beautiful singing voice was actually for turning up the volume on someone else's voice.

"You get the magic you're meant for," I say to Ginger now. "I guess you're just made for superficial magic." I shrug like it's no big deal, and like it's not a kind of mean thing to say. I wait for it to hurt her, but I don't think it does.

"Maddy said you'd be this way," Ginger says. "Bitter."

"I'm not bitter!" I say, but it comes out like a whine.

"We got what we were meant for," Ginger says, nodding her head toward Maddy, who is walking our way. "And you got what you were meant for." Her mouth curls into a little bit of a smile. Maybe her eyes look sad, maybe her eyes sort of miss me or wish one of us would stop being mean. But her mouth is happy to smile at Maddy and pretend I'm not there. She grabs Maddy's hand and the two of them walk toward their new best friend, Layla, and they all brush their fingers through their pink-streaked hair and pretend I don't exist.

I hate the way she's acting. But I hate the way I'm acting even more.

Twenty-five

A Story About the Friends I Used to Have

Six months ago, Ginger, Maddy, and I played Truth or Dare at Maddy's mom's house. She'd invited us over for a sleepover, and Ginger didn't want to go, but I thought it might be nice to swim in her pool, and sometimes I thought Maddy said something funny or smart or a little different than anything Ginger and I would have come up with, and I liked that.

Plus Maddy's mom let us watch whatever we wanted to on TV and sometimes made cookies and gave them to us fresh out of the oven. No one really cooked at my house.

And at Ginger's house there was only ever chicken fingers. I like chicken fingers and all, but not every weekend.

The three of us sat in Maddy's bedroom with a plate of cookies. Our hair was wet from the pool and the smell of chlorine was coming off every surface of our skin. The whole room smelled like chocolate and pool chemicals and sunscreen and I took out my sketch pad and started drawing us. I wanted to draw the way summer felt, the way friendship felt, the way it felt for it to be ten at night but not be in pajamas and for our hair to still be wet and to have our knees touching and the day never-ending.

"Maybe this is what capturing magic feels like," I said. I didn't know exactly what I meant, except that the night felt good and strange and brand-new.

I started with Ginger. I drew her long face and short hair and tiny nose and wide smile. I tried to make her hair look wet and her forehead look sweaty. I tried to make her smile look sleepy and her shoulders starting to sunburn. Maddy watched.

"Wow," she said. "You're good at that."

"Rose is good at everything," Ginger said.

"I'm only good at drawing," I said, laughing. I was very much *not* good at everything. I wasn't good at soccer like Ginger or diving like Maddy or being popular like Lyle. I was good at drawing. And magic. Supposedly.

175

"Well, you're *really* good at drawing," Maddy said. "Can you draw me next?"

I did. I added her to the picture of Ginger, sitting right next to her, cross-legged and leaning forward the way Maddy always did. Maddy never looked relaxed. She always looked like she was about to spring or jump or, I guess, dive. I drew her messy, knotted-up ponytail and how her swimsuit was a little too big for her shoulders.

"Add yourself too!" Maddy said. Ginger sighed. She had seen me draw a hundred million times; she didn't need to watch me show off now. But I couldn't help it. I loved the way Maddy's eyes were all lit up and how she'd point out which details in particular she liked the best. I drew myself in. My short, freckled legs. The big T-shirt I wore over my bathing suit and how the collar was all stretched out. The thick braids I'd quickly woven when we got out of the pool and the little drops of water sliding down my arms every so often from my wet hair.

"I thought we were playing Truth or Dare," Ginger said. "I wanted to get a dare."

Maddy seemed not to hear her. "Do you know how to draw boys, too?" Maddy asked. She had a sneaky smile and big eyes.

"I guess so," I said. I didn't draw boys ever. I drew me and Ginger. I drew cats with fairy wings and TooBlue Lake and our houses and gardens of wildflowers and enormous birthday cakes with confetti and candles on top. But I didn't see any reason that I wouldn't be able to draw boys.

"How about Evan Dell?" Maddy said.

I blushed. Evan Dell's name always made me blush. His eyes did too. And the way he laughed, with his head all the way back.

"Rose loooooooves Evan Dell," Ginger said.

"So does Ginger!" I said. Our voices were getting loud, and if we weren't careful Maddy's mom would get mad. Or maybe not. Maybe Maddy's mom didn't mind us being loud and silly past our bedtime.

"So do I!" Maddy exclaimed. She stood up when she said it, her hands on her hips like she was proud of it and not embarrassed, and for a minute I wondered what it would be like to be Maddy. I wanted a house with a pool and fresh-baked cookies and a dad who lived in one of the little houses in the center of town, who never got mad. I wanted to be the kind of person who didn't blush when they thought about Evan Dell or any other cute person.

So I drew. Ginger and Maddy kept correcting the shape of his head, the shade of his hair, the number of freckles on his nose. When I finally had a drawing we could all agree on, we fell asleep in a pile on the floor and woke up itchy and still tired and frizzy-haired and fresh from dreams about Evan Dell and his very blue eyes.

In the morning, we played Rock, Paper, Scissors for who got to keep the picture of Evan Dell, and Ginger won.

I didn't mind. I could draw a hundred pictures of Evan Dell if I wanted to, but there would only be that one perfect sleepover, that one best day of the summer. That one day that felt magical, even though it wasn't.

Twenty-six

Lunch at the cafeteria is fish sticks for most of us. Some people use their magic to change the fish sticks into turkey dinners and chocolate cakes, and I guess if you only catch silly magic, you can only do silly things. It feels to me like they're showing off how much magic they have, that they can use it on a random Tuesday at lunch without a second thought.

"This week will be the worst," Lyle said on our walk to school. "This will be the most magic, because it's new and exciting and people can't help themselves. You'll see. It will get better soon. By April a lot of them will have used up all their jars."

April feels a long way off right now. I'm sitting at a big

table all by myself, choking down cold fish sticks, which I'm drenching in mayonnaise to try to make them taste better. It doesn't really work.

Even Jamie Ollander with her allegedly dirty hair won't sit near me. She keeps glancing my way and sort of wincing, like it's painful to even look at me.

She caught seven jars of magic this year, so she's allowed to have a friend or two.

I'm lost in a moment of swirling my fish stick in mayonnaise and spreading some ketchup on top to see if that will help anything when I hear and feel someone sit down at the far end of the table. Two someones, actually. I look up to see who would dare, and it's Ginger. I start to smile at her. Then I see who she's sitting with. More than sitting with. Sitting very, very close to. Holding hands with. *Holding hands*. Ginger is holding hands with Evan Dell. She's leaning toward him and she is glancing at me like she wants to be sure I see, and obviously I do, everyone sees, because when someone is holding hands with someone else everyone notices and everyone talks about it and everyone wants to know if it means what we think it means.

Magic can't make people fall in love or anything. Dad was always really clear on that. Magic can do a lot of very cool things, but it can't control other people. It can change the weather and your eyelashes and what you're having for lunch. It can help you *find* someone to love. Or someone to be friends with. But it can't make someone feel something they don't already feel. It can't make someone different than who they are on the inside.

But of course, it can change some of the outside things that maybe Evan Dell likes. Hair and height and clothes and confidence. And Ginger has all of that now. She's taller, with longer hair and pink highlights and jeans with little hearts on the pockets. But she's also just so sure of herself. It could be any of those things that is making Evan Dell want to move a piece of pink hair from her face, offer her a drink of his soda, sit alone with her when all his friends are watching and snickering at their table without him.

I wonder if I was taller and pinker-haired and cooler-clothed, if Evan Dell would be holding my hand. My eyes feel like they want to cry, but I tell them no.

I can't stop thinking of the way Evan Dell used to be some boy we could giggle about and all think was cute and now he's Ginger's, and now she's some whole new person that I can't ever be. This isn't how it was supposed to be. I didn't think Evan Dell would ever be anyone but a cute boy I was good at drawing pictures of, and I didn't think Maddy would ever be anyone but an annoying sort-of-friend we tolerated together, and I didn't think Ginger and I would ever be anything but best best friends who did everything together.

The chair I'm sitting in is all cold and metal and these

stupid fish sticks are even colder and I'm tired of eating them and pretending it's all fine.

"Ginger, you must be so happy you finally got Evan Dell to talk to you," I say. I don't mean to say it. I was running through things I *could* say in my head, and that was one of the things I thought would be satisfying to say and somehow I thought it so hard that I said it out loud.

Ginger turns as pink as her hair and so does Evan Dell.

I can see her trying to think of something to say back, something that will embarrass me the way I've embarrassed her. Then I see her realize I can't get any more embarrassed than I've already been this week, so she just zips her mouth shut and glares at me.

I don't let her glare for long, though. I pick up my tray of soggy, condiment-covered fish sticks and leave that table and my old best friend and her new boyfriend or whatever he is. I'm getting used to storming away. Little Luck never needed to say mean things or stomp her feet or leave in a huff, but I'm not Little Luck anymore. I'm Rose Alice Anders, the biggest failure Belling Bright has ever seen, and I have nothing to lose.

And for one second that feels a little bit okay.

But only for one second.

Twenty-seven

Zelda's waiting for me. Maybe that's not actually what she's doing, sitting on the bench outside the rest stop, working on a dandelion chain, humming something that sounds made-up. Her hair's in a big pile on her head and it's all tangled up so it looks like a bird's nest, and Ginger and Maddy would probably make fun of it, but I love it. It looks like she cares more about dandelion crowns and stretching her legs out in the sun than she does about having shiny, straight, perfectly parted hair, and I want a little bit of whatever it is that she has.

I touch my own hair. I have bangs because Ginger got bangs and I was worried that soon everyone in the grade would have bangs and I wouldn't and they'd all be talking about me. I brush it in the mornings and worry about it all day long, carrying barrettes in my pockets and hairbands around my wrists in case Something Happens and I have a Hair Emergency, and it suddenly seems so ridiculous, to be worried about a strand of hair falling out of place.

"I love your hair," I say to Zelda instead of hello.

"Rose Alice Anders," she says. "You came back." She doesn't sound surprised at all.

"I didn't know where else to go."

She ties off her dandelion crown and places it atop her hair-nest. "What do you think?"

"It's perfect," I say.

"I can make you one."

"Okay," I say. "It won't look as—it won't look the same on me."

Zelda squints. "Well, of course not," she says. "We don't look the same at all."

"Well—right. But like, it won't be as cool." I blush. I'm not making any sense at all. I'm trying to compliment her and it's coming out all jumbled and weird.

Zelda shrugs. She wiggles her toes. I somehow notice her wiggling her toes before I notice that I can *see* her toes, which means she's barefoot.

"My father likes to be barefoot, too," I say. "It helps him with the magic."

"Oh," Zelda says. She's thinking. She thinks for what feels like a while. "Well, that's definitely not why I like being barefoot." She smiles. "I just like being outside. And being barefoot means my feet are outside, too. You know?"

I don't know, but I nod like I do. It's sort of weird, but it's always felt like Dad owned being barefoot. Like that was a thing he invented. But here's Zelda, coming up with her own reasons to be barefoot.

It shouldn't be weird, but it is weird, and that's what makes it so weird.

She finishes the crown for me quickly and puts it on my head. It feels light. I feel lighter, too.

"I thought you might be back," Zelda says.

"You did?"

"Well, hoped, I guess." Zelda smiles. It's big and bright. She doesn't look embarrassed even though it's the kind of thing that would embarrass me to say. I'm embarrassed by how much I wanted to see Zelda today. "We don't talk to lots of people. Especially not, you know, you guys."

"Is it weird that I'm here? Mom says I shouldn't go any-where I'm not invited."

"I don't know anything about that rule, so it's fine with

me," Zelda says. "What other rules do you have?"

There are so many I don't know where to start. "We try to be quiet if Dad's sleeping," I say. "We don't touch the jars of magic. We—I don't know. We try to be good all the time."

"All the time sounds like a lot of time to be good," Zelda says. She's right. It is so, so, so much time to try to be good. It's suddenly impossible that no one's ever said that before. It's so obvious. No one's good all the time.

Especially if what it means to be good changes sometimes.

"I'm sort of failing at it," I say. "My dad thinks the goodest thing you can do is get a bunch of magic."

"I guess I'm pretty awful, then," Zelda says. She smiles again, but it's a smaller smile. "It's not so bad, you know."

"What isn't so bad?"

"Being Not Meant for Magic. That's why you're here, right? To see what it's like?" Zelda starts in on another crown. There's no one else here to give it to, but someone like Zelda could probably wear a dozen flower crowns at once and look like it was always meant to be that way.

"I don't know why I'm here," I say. It's easier to tell Zelda the truth than anyone else right now.

"You want to make a dandelion necklace?" Zelda says, like maybe that's the reason. And maybe it is.

"Sure."

Zelda gets off the bench and bends down to the grass. There are a zillion dandelions under our feet. Whoever did the Spring magic made it strong and fast, weeds and flowers and trees growing and blossoming all around us, as if winter never happened. She pulls two huge fistfuls of dandelions and we get to work. I try to do it exactly the way she's doing, making my hands mirror hers. When Zelda notices, she shakes her head.

"This is just how I do it," she says.

"I want to do it the way you do it," I say.

"But then it won't be yours." Zelda squints and cocks her head. I think about all the years of trying to be just like my father. I was *sure* that if I imitated his rituals and used all his tips and had his bare feet and his lucky scarf, I'd be as good at capturing magic as he is. Even if I felt a bunch of things in my heart that he never felt.

"In town, we'd make these out of magic," I say. "They'd be different colors, or bigger, or they'd have glitter shooting out of them or something."

"Then they wouldn't really be dandelion crowns anymore," Zelda says. She shakes her head and looks up at the sun, then at me. "Magic's so weird. I don't get it."

"But it's everywhere," I say. "Like every kid anywhere around here just waits to turn twelve and we all have lists of

187

all the different things we could do with it, and we change all kinds of things from the magic, we make things better and ourselves happier and—I mean, even the way the sky looks right now might be from someone's magic. These dandelions. The fact that winter is gone and it's January and we're outside making these crowns. Magic is—it's everything and everywhere all the time."

"Well. It's not here," Zelda says. "Even when Mom and Dad said Lucy and I could go try to capture it—I don't know. It seemed sort of weird."

"Weird to make the world better?" I ask. I wish I could put on Zelda-glasses and see the world the way she does.

"There's a lot of non-magical ways to make the world better," she says.

She sounds so sure, but I've only ever thought of magical ones. Still, I like the idea that I could still do something good, even without one hundred sixty-one jars of magic to help me do it.

"You sort of look like Lucy," Zelda says out of nowhere, but I'm trying to keep up, so I just nod.

"I guess," I say.

Zelda isn't bothered by silence, so we sit in it, the silence, and make dandelion necklaces. Hers are better than mine. And I keep trying to imitate her fingers and she keeps shaking her head when she catches me doing it.

"Dad says we have to find our own way," she says.

There's something different about the things her dad tells her about the world and how to be in it and the things my dad's told me. Just like there's something different about what it means that Zelda likes to be barefoot and what it means that my dad does.

"How did you know you weren't meant for magic?" I ask. I try to say it casually, like it's no big deal if she answers or not and I don't really care what her answer is anyway.

But in the pause between my asking and her answering, I realize I do actually care.

"I guess it never felt like something I needed. And it seems silly to spend all that time and effort on something I don't actually need." She makes it sound so easy. Like magic is an accessory. That's not how Dad makes it sound, when he talks about it. And it was so easy to get caught up in his excitement. Dad's excitement is bubbly and fun and big and beautiful. It's easy to get caught up in.

"What do your parents think about magic?" I ask.

"Don't you know all this?" Zelda asks. It's a funny question.

"I don't know anything," I say, because I only just learned about being Not Meant for Magic, and I only just met Zelda and her family. But Zelda looks at me like *I'm* the one saying kind of wacky stuff, not her, and she puts down all her dandelions to look right at me.

"My dad decided we weren't meant for magic," Zelda says. "He did it for a while. Went to TooBlue Lake. I guess he was even sort of good at all the magic stuff—"

"The capturing."

"Sure. The capturing. But then when he was a little older, he just—couldn't."

"Couldn't capture magic anymore?" Zelda is speaking so vaguely, and I want to know everything. I've never heard a story of someone who stopped capturing magic.

"Or wouldn't?" Zelda says, like there's no important difference between the two. "I don't know. He said that magic is really beautiful. And does beautiful things. But that it's fake beautiful. And it made people sort of . . . fake beautiful too."

I'd think I'd have a bunch of questions about this idea. But instead it feels like Zelda is answering something I've always known.

"So he just . . . gave it up?" I ask.

"He stopped believing in the things you have to believe in, to capture magic," she says.

"Oh."

I think about the things my father says and how I don't always believe in them the way I'm supposed to. And the way he ran on the deserted beach like he'd done it before, like he'd done it many times before, like the rules weren't really for him. I think about Ginger's pink hair and Evan Dell's fingers intertwined with hers.

And I think, for one half second, about my family and all the times Lyle and I have gone to the roof together to get away from things.

I think about the jar of UnTired magic Dad opened on us all. That it didn't help anything and we didn't want it and my mom was actually a little scared of it, and if magic goes where it's supposed to go, why did that jar go to him?

Why do any of the jars?

Zelda puts another crown on her head. I put another bracelet around my wrist. My fingers are tired from twisting and braiding and knotting. My head is tired from thinking. If I had magic, I would have made real crowns with rhinestones; I would have hoped for magic that could make roses and violets grow where dandelions were.

But maybe that would have been wrong.

"Do you ever want to go into town?" I ask. I didn't know this place was here, and I wonder how little Zelda knows about us, where we live, what our Belling Bright is like.

"I'm in town right now," Zelda says.

"Oh. Right. But like, *in* town. Where everyone else is. There's a big birthday party this weekend and I thought maybe you'd want to come," I say. It's a bad idea. Zelda thinks magic is fake, and if she says yes to my big idea, she'll be surrounded by all the fake beautiful magic that she hates.

But I love the way she sees the world and the quiet and maybe-true things she tells me about it. I like being near her and who I am when I'm talking to her.

"Oh! More people!" Zelda says. Her eyes light up. She doesn't care about all the magic that will probably be there, like magical sunsets or magical bouncy houses or magical cakes that Ginger's family magicked up one year that had flavors like Summer Breeze or Christmas Morning or You've Finished Everything You Had to Do That You Didn't Want to Do. What Zelda wants to see is other people. I can tell from the way her eyes look suddenly dreamy, her mouth bright with wondering. "Will there be lots of other people there? Like, how many do you think?"

"Oh, tons. Maybe a hundred? Or more? Anyone in town who feels like it, I guess."

"A hundred people," Zelda says. Her smile doesn't fade. Her eyes don't dim. "I've always wanted to meet a hundred people."

"Really?"

"Are they your friends?" she asks. "Do you watch movies and play Monopoly and tell secrets?"

"I guess we do those things," I say. And as we talk, I see something new about Zelda. Maybe no one really comes by this rest stop. Maybe they know the people who run it are Not Meant for Magic. "Do you have friends?" I ask, even though it seems sort of rude. Zelda seems like a person who doesn't really mind rudeness.

"Just my family," Zelda says. "No one wants to be friends with us."

"Maybe if you went to a less magical town?" I ask, thinking there must be friends for Zelda somewhere.

"Oh," she says. "We'd never do that."

"Why not?"

She gives me a look like it's obvious. "Family," she says. "We have to stay close, to keep an eye on our family."

It seems like they could keep an eye on each other anywhere they went, but I don't say that because I think it would sound rude. Plus, I don't want Zelda and her family to leave Belling Bright. I love having them here.

"Well, you have me to be friends with now," I say. I say it because I want it to be true, and because maybe Zelda will want it to be true, and if two people want it to be true, doesn't that make it true?

"Yes," Zelda says. "And this weekend maybe I'll have even more friends!"

"Oh," I say, my heart sinking at the thought of everyone liking Zelda more than me. "Maybe."

"But it wouldn't be the same as it is with you," she says.

"It wouldn't?"

"Of course not," Zelda says. And she gives me another

smile, one that looks like we are in on a secret, which maybe we are, because Zelda is the only secret I've ever kept from my father.

I don't know exactly what fake beautiful is. But I know this moment is a certain kind of beautiful, the way that perfect summer day at Maddy's house was beautiful.

And if I had magic, it never would have happened at all.

Twenty-eight

"This isn't a conversation," Mom says.

"This is definitely a conversation," I say. "We're talking right now, back and forth."

"She means it isn't a negotiation," Lyle says. He's at the kitchen counter helping Mom make pasta salad by chopping up celery and whisking vinegar with oil, and I should be helping too, except I can't seem to put down Ginger's birthday party invitation.

"I'm bringing Zelda," I say. Every year, Ginger's family throws a birthday party for her. Or, not just for her. For all of them. Ginger and all of her siblings and also her mom. And when her dad was here, for him too. They all have birthdays in the winter months, and instead of trying to throw nine different birthday parties, they throw one big one. They save up their magic for it. They choose which jars seem the most likely to be able to make perfect weather and a delicious meal, and every year there's something unexpected and thrilling, a bit of magic no one knew about.

Last year it was a lemonade fountain. The year before that there were pony rides on pink and purple ponies. And before that there was the biggest bouncy house I've ever seen. Bigger than any house in town. It played musical notes on every bounce, making the whole thing extra loud and extra fun and extra magical.

Ginger and I used to like to make lists of things that might happen, trying to imagine which jars might have the strangest magic, which jars might hold something we'd never seen or heard of before. Ginger and I had so many traditions it's hard to escape them. They pop up like weeds everywhere I look.

Even what we're cooking right now is a tradition. On top of whatever the magic makes, the rest of us bring food to the party. We always bring non-magical pasta salad. Mom says it tastes better without magic. Dad never helps us make it. I'm not sure he ever eats it.

"I told you to forget about that girl," Mom says. "And now you want to bring her to your best friend's birthday party? What's gotten into you?"

"She's not my best friend anymore."

"Well, bringing Zelda wouldn't help that at all."

"She has a new best friend that isn't me. So I need a best friend, too. And no one wants to be best friends with one-jar girl. Especially not Ginger. She even has a boyfriend to go along with her new life." I hadn't meant to tell Mom about Evan Bell, and even thinking about him makes my insides all cloudy and pinchy.

"Ginger has a boyfriend?" Lyle says. He starts to laugh.

"It's not funny," I say.

"It's a little funny," Lyle says.

"It's not about whether or not Ginger needs you," Mom says. "Although I'm sure she does. It's about living our lives. It's about you still being you, no matter what happened. We can't go changing everything around just because you had a hard start to the year."

Mom hands me the bowl of ingredients to stir, and I do. Lyle keeps shaking his head and laughing about Ginger and her boyfriend. Outside, the sky is turning bluer and bluer and bluer. It had been a gray day when we woke up, but not anymore. The magic has begun.

"Life without magic is—well. It's nice, but it's not for us. And it's too confusing to invite Zelda." When Mom says the word *nice* she looks like she really means it. She actually looks like she means more than nice. Like she means special or beautiful or *better.*

But she doesn't want to talk about it.

197

It shouldn't surprise me, that Mom wants to pretend nothing is happening, that everything's fine.

"That's one blue sky," Dad says. He's coming in from outside, where he's been practicing his capturing moves, I guess. His feet are bare and he's got a line of sweat over his lip and on his forehead. "Warm too," he says. "They got some strong magic this year, that's for sure."

I wonder if he sees how the words puncture me. It's impossible not to talk about magic when it's still January and we live in Belling Bright and the sky is turning blue and the air is turning warm and delicious, the way only magic can make it feel. But still, I wish we could talk about anything else.

"Beautiful day," Mom says. All the words are normal, but *I'm* not normal, which makes the words sound weird.

"Fake beautiful," I say. I don't know what makes me say it exactly. Especially in front of Dad. But once the words are out they can't exactly go anywhere else, so we're all stuck with them. We shift around. Mom swallows so loudly I can hear it. Lyle stares at his feet. Dad just stares at me.

"Where'd you hear that?" he says at last.

"Hear what?"

"'Fake beautiful.' Who said that to you?"

"No one," I say. "I just meant that like, the sky isn't *really* blue. It's magically blue. So it's not . . . it's not like a surprise or really special. It's just magic." I hadn't thought out the words ahead of time, but when I say them they feel true, truer than that blue sky at least, and that's something.

"Magic isn't special now?" Dad says.

"I just mean it would be even cooler if the sky just did this on its own."

"Why?" Dad asks. Mom and Lyle stir and chop and clear their throats. "What would make that better? Would it be prettier? Blue is blue, Rose."

"It would be real," I say.

"Not fake," Dad says.

"Yes. Not fake beautiful." He reacts again to those particular words in that particular order. He looks at Mom.

"Why is she saying that?" he asks. His voice is strained, like it's pushing up against something.

"I don't know, Wendell," Mom says.

"She didn't just come up with it on her own," he says.

"Who knows where Rose comes up with these things," Mom says, but her voice shakes and her eyes dart around and anyone could tell she's hiding something. I know what she's hiding. What I don't know is how those two words made Dad figure it out.

"You went there," he says. He says it to Mom. Then he turns to me. "She took you there." The part of him that was tired is gone, and now only the anger is left. "That's why I didn't want you taking them there. They get confused. They get— I told you not to. Not ever."

"It was an accident," Mom says.

"An accident!" Dad says. He laughs, like it's a joke, but it's a bad laugh, a mean laugh, and clearly not a joke at all. "You've always wanted this. You've always hated what I do, what I care about."

"I wasn't thinking," Mom says. "It was after Rose— It was when we left TooBlue Lake and we were all out of sorts and we needed coffee and food and it was open and I thought, I don't know, that maybe Rose would feel better knowing that not everyone in Belling Bright uses magic to do everything, and I thought it would be good for the kids to meet—"

I watch Mom try to find the rest of the sentence, but she can't. She keeps looking at the pasta, at the window, at Lyle. And by the time she looks at Dad, she seems nervous and sorry and ready to say whatever Dad wants her to say. Except she doesn't say anything.

"They were nice," I say, before Mom can say something or not say something and make Dad even madder. "It wasn't a big deal. I liked them. And the girl—Zelda—she's cool. That's where I heard that phrase. I guess her dad says it. I didn't mean— It's just a thing she said, so I said it, but I didn't mean anything by it."

Dad turns to me. He's red-faced. He shakes his head. I wait for his anger to turn to me, but he only lingers on my face for a second before turning back to Mom.

"We agreed," he says. "We promised we'd live— Zelda. What a name. *Zelda*. Sounds like him."

"Like who?" I ask.

"You will not go back there," Dad says.

"Zelda sounds like who?" I ask again.

"Zelda's father and I—we don't get along. I knew him, a long time ago," Dad says. "I don't want you seeing that girl anymore. I don't want you parroting the ridiculous garbage she's telling you. We are the Anders family of Belling Bright and we are meant for magic and we live right here, in town, and we don't go traipsing out to some rest stop where who knows what is happening. Do you hear me, Rose Alice Anders?"

"I hear you," I say. And it's not a lie, because I do. I hear him.

But I'm not going to listen.

Twenty-nine

What I'm Thinking About
While I Wait for Zelda in the Center of Town
Even Though Dad Said No

Ginger came over for my eleventh birthday last year.
It wasn't how we usually did things. But I'd begged my
mother and she'd begged my father and Lyle was fine with
whatever, so we broke with tradition and had Ginger sitting
there for cake and the remembering of the day I was born.

"You do this every year?" she asked. "Tell the same
story? Eat the same foods?"

"It's luck," I said.

"What about the magic?" Ginger asked.

"What magic?" Dad asked. He was grumpy. He didn't
like changes, especially before New Year's Day. Mom said it

made him nervous, the way baseball players wear the same socks for every game. But that didn't make any sense. If magic knew what it was doing, he shouldn't need superstitions.

"Don't you do special magic for Rose's birthday?" Ginger asked. She looked around the room like a rainbow might explode out of the wall or we all might suddenly grow wings or something.

"We don't do things the way your family does them," Dad said.

"Wendell," Mom said, her voice a warning.

"Well, it's true. You're in our home, you should respect our ways of doing things," Dad said. He'd never spoken to Ginger that way. Usually he treated me and Ginger like we were a package deal, his two girls.

"I just meant since you have so much magic, you could really do almost anything, so for birthdays—" Ginger stopped herself when she saw the look on my father's face.

"Magic is serious," he said. "Maybe your parents didn't teach you that."

Ginger's face collapsed. Her body too. Her shoulders slumped. She'd always loved my father, and with her father sick she'd been coming around more and more. "I guess we don't talk about magic much at home," Ginger whispered.

"Of course not, sweetheart," Mom said. "You have a lot going on. And magic is—"

"Magic is everything," Dad interrupted. "I'm working right now on magic for your father. For other fathers. And mothers. For people all over this town. They come to me. They want my help. They need to learn how to use their magic or they beg to borrow some of ours. Except it's not borrowing, is it, because they're not giving it back. You think the magic just appears? That we should waste it on a bunch of silliness like everyone else? I watch the people of this town waste their magic on making themselves look good, making their puppies talk for an hour, growing pineapples crossed with broccoli in their magical gardens. And then at the end of the day, all that magic's been used up, and they're counting on me to fix everything. They think I'm—they don't respect the way I do things until they need me. Does that seem fair to you?"

I didn't know for sure who he was talking to then. He wasn't looking at Ginger or even Mom. He wasn't looking at me and Lyle.

"Thanks for helping," Ginger muttered, but she didn't mean it. I knew when Ginger meant something and when she didn't.

"We all need some rest," Mom said. "Right, Wendell?"

My father didn't reply. He stormed upstairs and Mom followed and they didn't come back downstairs. They didn't finish their cake or the story of the day I was born.

Lyle cut himself an extra piece and offered some to each

of us. I shook my head, so Ginger shook hers, but Lyle gave us some anyway. "It's still your birthday," he said. And he was right, even though it had never felt less like my birthday.

"That was scary," Ginger said when we'd been in silence a few minutes longer.

"He's got a big responsibility," I said. "He doesn't need any more pressure."

"He's never like that," Lyle said.

"Tomorrow's really important," I said.

"I—" Ginger said.

"You should probably call your mom and go home," I said. I didn't intend it to come out meanly. But I needed her gone. I needed her out of the house and out of this moment and maybe to forget any of this ever happened.

"I—" Ginger said. She shook her head. She hung it. She tucked her hair behind her ears. "Okay."

"It's okay," I said, "I'm not mad."

Ginger looked at me extra hard, extra long. "Mad," she said, and it wasn't a question or a statement. I don't know what it was. It was a break in the thing between us, a moment where we weren't two peas in a pod anymore, the exact moment in time when things started to change, even though I didn't know it and didn't understand it and definitely couldn't stop it.

When she was gone, I helped Lyle do the dishes.

"Happy birthday," he said.

"I'm scared," I said.

"There's nothing to be scared of."

"There's not?"

"Everything's fine."

"It is?"

"Everyone has hard days," Lyle said. He sounded so sure. Like he was really and truly the big brother that he'd always been. He said it like I could trust him and also like I needed to trust him, so I did.

I tried.

"Everything's fine," I said, to myself and to him, and to Ginger the next day and to everyone who asked ever again.

Thirty

Zelda looks strange, standing in the center of town with her overalls and toothy smile, not worrying about what anyone's thinking.

"We should go to your place," I say instead of hello. I want to get her out of here, away from my father and away from everyone. I want to go back to that perfect sunny moment with dandelion crowns and no one looking at us.

"No way," Zelda says. "Look at all these people! Are they all your friends? What are their names? Can you introduce me to them?" Zelda is rosy-cheeked and beaming, seeing a town full of people. I want to believe they'd like her, if they got to know her, but after the fight with my father, I know that's not possible. Belling Bright doesn't like people who don't like magic. There isn't room for someone like Zelda here.

"They used to be my friends," I say. "But we don't need them. All they care about is magic. It's not— Whatever you think it is, it isn't that way. I made a mistake. I shouldn't have invited you." The center of town is filling up with party-goers, and all of them are looking at Zelda, looking at me, looking back at Zelda again.

I look at Zelda too. Her smile's gone. "Oh," she says. "You wish I hadn't come."

"No," I say, "I just like where you live. I want to get to know your parents. And your sister. And I want to get better at dandelion crowns. And I want to be . . . not here."

She nods. But she doesn't say okay, doesn't start walking the mile to the rest stop.

"And I want to get to know your parents and your life and these people," she says, like it's the most obvious thing in the world. "I don't know anyone. I don't see anyone. No one—people avoid our place and we avoid them and—can we stay a little while? I just want to see how people—what it looks like, to have all these people in one place. To be a part of it."

I can't help loving how Zelda doesn't pretend she's fine. She doesn't pretend at all, I think. I wonder what that's like.

My dad won't be here for a while. We can stay for a moment; then maybe she'll see how much Ginger's changed and how sneaky Maddy is and how cute Evan Dell is and how shocking it is that he's Ginger's boyfriend. Maybe she'll see the way they look at me—like they're happy I failed—and maybe she'll have some way to make me feel better about it. I let myself believe that if I let her see Belling Bright, I won't feel so alone in it anymore.

"Okay," I say. "Let's stay for a little."

Zelda beams. "Thank you," she says. "I just want to— know what it's like."

I try to see it through her eyes, but it's impossible. These are just people and this is just a party and it's all just Belling Bright, the same as it's always been. I'm what's different and new.

There are tables set up with all different kinds of food. Baked goods and fruits and cheeses and miniature sandwiches with nothing but cucumber and butter inside. It's the same every year. There's delicious cake, and some high school band plays songs that we all sort of half know, and Ginger's mother tries to get us started on a bunch of games that I'm never interested in but somehow always end up playing. Freeze tag. Hide-and-seek. Hopscotch. Kickball.

"It's exactly how I imagined it," Zelda says. "All these people. Having fun. But where's all the magic?"

"Everywhere," I say. Zelda's looking for something specific, and that will happen too, but magic is everywhere, always, and especially right now. "Her hair," I say, pointing

209

to a woman with intricate braids who used to have chin-length hair a few days ago. "That tree. Those shoes. The temperature. The way the air smells." I pause. The clock in the center of town chimes out. Greggor Barnum is using his magic to tell us the time. "The way people seem happy. That's magic. The things they're talking about. What they remember of last year's party. Magic. All of it is magic."

"Just—everything?" Zelda asks. "Isn't that confusing?"

"Confusing?"

"Like, how do you know what's real and what's magical?"

"It's all magical," I say.

"Except for you, maybe," Zelda says with a smile that tells me she doesn't know those words sting me.

She's saying things and I'm saying things, but we aren't really having the same conversation, I don't think. I can't explain how magic makes everything work, how it's not just the cake and the balloons and the weather. That it's also the way we walk around, it's why no one has the sniffles today, it's the angle of the sun in the sky. It's everything.

Except Zelda's right too. It's everything except me. And her.

"If you'd gotten more magic, what would you have used it on?" Zelda's never asked much about my magic. Or maybe I've never let her. It's hard to say.

"I guess the same things Ginger's using hers on. Hair. Clothes. Math. It's sort of silly, I guess."

"Not silly," Zelda says. She sounds like she's thinking really hard.

"What would you have used your magic on?" I ask Zelda. I bet she would think of something amazing, and that she's the kind of person who would capture important and beautiful magic. The kind that could help a sick cat or make you really good at painting or turn weeds into violets or something.

"I wouldn't use magic," Zelda says.

"No, I know you're Not Meant for Magic, but if you were, what would you do?" I ask.

Zelda tilts her head and shakes it. "I wouldn't," she says again. "Even if—even if I went to the lake with you and captured something, I guess I'd just let it back out. Like the way my dad does when he goes fishing."

We walk under a canopy made of streamers, and I watch it for signs of magic. Maybe it will sing or light up or move around in some beautiful way. Maybe the streamers will perform a dance. Or change colors. Or float into the sky like fireworks. But they stay put.

"So which one is Ginger?" Zelda asks.

I point to my old best friend.

"With the yellow dress?"

"Yes." I'd noticed how much more pink is in Ginger's hair, how much longer it is, how straight her back is, her big smile. I hadn't noticed the dress, but it's one I've never seen before. It's got skinny straps and orange flowers and it waves around her knees like it's dancing there. I squint and it shimmers. Magic. The rest of Ginger's clothes are from the secondhand shop downtown and from her brothers and sisters. She's always wanted a brand-new dress, and I'm happy she has one now. For a moment, I'm not jealous. I'm just happy for Ginger, who looks pretty and calm and more like a birthday girl than she's ever looked at one of these parties. She hugs people hello and practically seems to be glittering herself. Or levitating. She might be levitating.

"Huh," Zelda says. "She isn't anything like you."

It isn't meant as anything—not a compliment or an insult. Zelda says everything like it's a fact, and I don't like that this might be a fact now, too. The jealousy comes back, landing right in my throat, where it squeezes and then speaks. Zelda is seeing something I've been afraid is true. That not only do I not fit into Belling Bright, but I don't belong to Ginger anymore either, or my family, or myself. I don't belong anywhere or to anyone, and everyone—even someone who has never left her little home on the outskirts of town before—can see it.

"We have a ton in common," I say. "We've been—we *were*—best friends forever. We like all the same foods and colors and singers and books."

"I'm not talking about that kind of thing," Zelda says.

"Well, what are you talking about, then?" I ask. My

voice is starting to break a little on the edges—all of me is starting to shatter and fall apart, really, and the closer Ginger gets the shakier I am until she's right in front of me and Zelda's hand is on my shoulder, which isn't an answer to my question but is something else I needed much, much more.

"I'm glad you're here," Ginger says right away. She pulls me in for a hug. Then it's over and I miss it.

I almost say: *My mom said I had to come,* but I realize just in time that just because that's true doesn't mean it's nice or worth saying.

"I like your dress," I say instead, which is true enough. I like it. Maybe not as much as I'd like it if I could have one of my own, but the dress reminds me of spring and gardens, and that's something, too.

"I like your—" She looks me over. She's looking for something about me to like. Something that seems magical or worthy or just *okay.* She comes up short. "You brought a friend," she says instead.

"Zelda," I say.

"Zelda. Hi. You're from . . . ?" Ginger is having trouble finishing a sentence.

"The rest stop," Zelda says. "Right on the edge of town."

"Oh. Okay. The rest stop at the edge of town. I'll have to check it out." Ginger's mouth is doing a funny thing. It's hiding something. I look closer, to see what's underneath. A smirk. She's hiding a smirk. There's a meanness to it.

"We'd love to have you!" Zelda says. Zelda's mouth isn't hiding anything. I wonder if Zelda's mouth has ever hidden anything. Maybe not. Maybe she doesn't know how to.

"It's not just a rest stop," I say. "They have a house."

"Well. That's good," Ginger says. She's doing worse at hiding the smirk.

"A really nice house," I say.

"We're Not Meant for Magic," Zelda says. The words shoot out of her before I have a chance to stop them.

Ginger's eyebrows dart up as far as they can go and maybe a little bit higher. They look like they hurt, hanging out up there. Then she looks at me. She tilts her head.

"*You're* Not Meant for Magic?" she asks me.

I'm going to answer. I mean to answer. An answer is definitely brewing inside of me, but before I have a chance to let it out, Zelda answers for me. "We're not sure about Rose yet," she says. "Maybe!"

"Wow. Well. That would explain a lot," Ginger says. Her smirk is all the way out, and now she's hiding a laugh. A big one. Maddy flies up to us and gives Ginger a hug, and the hug shrivels up whatever okay-ness was left in me.

"I have my jar," I mumble. But no one hears me. Maddy and Ginger sort of lean against each other. I remember that lean. The way it felt to have Ginger's shoulder against mine. How it was bony and cool. How it felt, sometimes, like it was part of my body, like we were the same person.

I try leaning against Zelda now, but she moves too quickly, too often for it to work. She fidgets. She shifts her weight every second. Her shoulder is only her shoulder. It's not something I know or love or recognize. It's just a shoulder.

"I'm so curious what you're going to use your jar for," Maddy says. "You'll have to let us know."

I shrug. There are probably a hundred ways I could respond to this, but I can't come up with them. And before I have a chance to linger on it, Maddy's pulling Ginger away and the two of them are running toward Evan Dell and his friends and Zelda is smiling after them and I'm just here, watching streamers wave in the sky, watching balloons bounce on strings, wondering what here is magic and what here is not, and knowing mostly that I am the thing that is not.

Thirty-one

"We should go," I say. "There's not much else to see. And my parents will be here soon." I want to say other things too. That she shouldn't have said I might not be Meant for Magic. That we should have stayed at her house and not come out into town together. That I'm not ready to not care about magic and that a big part of me still wishes my life was the one I was supposed to have instead of this one.

But mostly I just want to get out of here.

"They will?" Zelda's eyes light up. "Like, your dad will be here?" I'm used to people wanting to meet my father, but it doesn't seem quite right for Zelda, who doesn't care about how many jars he's caught and how powerful the magic in his jars usually is.

"In a little bit," I say. "And we should leave before he is."

"Why would we do that?"

"Oh, well, they don't really want me hanging out with you. My dad especially. I'm not really supposed to—he doesn't like it."

Zelda's face clouds. "He doesn't want me around?" she whisper-asks. "He doesn't want to meet me?"

"Why would he want to meet you?" I whisper-ask back.

"I thought maybe—after all this time—and how well we get along—and everything that's happened with you—I thought maybe he'd finally—" She doesn't get a chance to finish her sentence because there's an explosion of laughter so loud I have to look over to where everyone else is looking.

The laughter is coming from Ginger and Evan Dell. They're standing together, and Ginger's laugh is a little bit nervous and a little bit forced. Evan Dell's is loud. Then louder. Then he's calling his friends over. "Ryan! Ashton! Garrett! Come here! You gotta see this!"

"Oh, it's not— I don't think we should show everyone," I hear Ginger saying.

"This is so funny!" Evan Dell says, laughing harder still.

My heart pounds. I don't know why, exactly, except that Ginger's laugh is usually light and easy, the kind of thing that pours out of her. And her laugh right now keeps getting stuck on its way out of her mouth, so it sounds like little hiccups in the middle of her giggles.

217

"Are you okay?" Zelda asks.

"What are they laughing at?" I ask, because my hands have found their way to my face and I can't bear to move my fingers away from my eyes. Whatever is happening, I don't want to see it.

"A piece of paper?" Zelda says, asking it like a question, which makes sense because there's nothing very funny about a piece of paper. "And— Oh! The magic! Something's happening!"

"What's on the piece of paper?" I ask, but I think some part of me knows.

"You have to open your eyes, Rose!" Zelda says, not hearing my question or not understanding that I've seen magic a hundred times, but I've never seen Ginger have a boyfriend. I've never heard Ginger laugh like that. "It's—it's incredible." Zelda grabs my hands and pulls them from my eyes. I know what she wants me to see: there's a jar in the center of the party that has been opened. And exploding out of it is water, except the water is pink and purple and green. Everyone runs to stand under the magical water fountain. The temperature of the air goes up in an instant, a magical heat wave that makes the magical water fountain even better. Zelda gives a little gasp-shriek that none of the rest of us do, because the water is pretty and the heat feels good, but magic isn't anything new, isn't really all that magical at all, anymore.

I see the water. I feel the heat. I watch Maddy and Layla run under the water first and everyone else follows. When the pink and purple and green reaches their skin, it turns them into rainbow-people, for a moment, then they return to their normal selves. It's pretty. It's strange. It's exactly the kind of magic Ginger's family hopes for every year.

But I don't care about any of it. Because I see what's in Evan Dell's hands. It's a thick piece of construction paper with a pencil drawing on it. The drawing is of Evan Dell himself. It couldn't be anyone else. It is exactly his head and exactly his eyes and exactly his mouth drawn by someone who has spent a lot a lot a lot of time thinking about Evan Dell's head and eyes and mouth. There is a border of hearts around the perfect drawing of perfect Evan Dell. And the artist has signed her name. Because she was told, once, that real artists sign their name to even the silliest doodles they draw in case they are famous one day.

And the artist thought maybe she'd be famous one day, because she already sort of was.

Rose Alice Anders, the drawing says, in my loopy hand-writing, which is always crooked and always messy and always, always, big enough for anyone who sees the picture to read.

Zelda runs herself right into the fountain of rainbow-colored water and grins at the way her arms turn neon pink and forest green and royal blue. She lifts her hands up and up and up, like she wants to capture magic, right here and now, even though she's not meant for it, even though she doesn't believe in it and doesn't like it and has spent her whole life hearing about how silly and fake it all is.

Her hair turns all kinds of colors, too, orange and yellow and a sparkly bronze. She shakes it off and rainbow-colored droplets fly from her head and land all over the lawn.

Rainbow drops are flying everywhere, colors I've heard of but never seen flying through the air. But I can't see anything except for that stupid picture I drew for Ginger and Maddy, when everything in the world seemed safe and sure and fine, when Evan Dell was cute in a far-off, distant way, when Ginger was my friend and magic was mine to capture and there wasn't a girl with dandelion crowns and long arms and a face a little like mine who said strange and mysterious things.

It feels like a long time ago, but it wasn't that long ago.

But also it was forever ago. Because now Ginger won't look at me, and Evan Dell and his friends won't stop looking at me, and my dad is here and he is looking right at Zelda.

Thirty-two

I run.

I'm getting good at running. I'm getting fast, which is saying something, because it's Ginger who is good at sports and running, and I'm not really much good at anything, it turns out, except for drawing the exact shape of Evan Dell's nose.

I'm good at running, but Dad is better because Dad has magic. And when he catches up with me we are halfway between the party and our home, which just happens to be the school playground, a place no one plays in anymore because a playground isn't so interesting when you have magic to experiment with and crushes to think about and friends to make miserable and mysterious girls on the edge of town to befriend.

Zelda's fast too and she's right behind us, the tops of her hair still golden-green from the magical water.

We're in silence, all of us, looking out at the path we drew with our fast feet, looking for Mom and Lyle to spring up too, but they're nowhere to be seen. Maybe they want to stand under the magical waterfall and forget about me and the trouble I've caused.

It's just me, Dad, and the one person Dad told me to stay away from only a few hours ago.

"I'm trying to understand," Dad says, but he doesn't look like someone trying to understand. His hair is messy from his hands traveling through it and pulling at it; he is red-faced from the run over here or his feelings, I can't be sure. He keeps rubbing his forehead, and I know that's never a good sign with him. It's what he does before he does something else or says something else or gives me more memories I want to forget all about.

"That's what *I'm* doing!" I say. "*I'm* trying to understand! You didn't tell me this was a possibility. You didn't tell me I might fail. You didn't tell me how to be out in the world without being Little Luck. You didn't tell me there were people who were Not Meant for Magic. And you did not tell me I might be one of them!" I fling my arms all around. Then I feel like Dad, the way he sometimes is, and that makes me want to still my arms.

"You didn't tell her about us," Zelda says.

"She didn't need to know about people who are Not Meant for Magic," Dad says. "How would that help her? And she isn't— She caught a jar. She got scared or distracted or who knows what, but there's no reason to start worrying about—"

"He didn't tell you who we are," Zelda says. She keeps looking at my father like they both know something big that I don't know.

"I know who you are," I say, but the words don't feel true, and Zelda's face is hard and the temperature is starting to drop, the party is already ending, the magic is running out.

"Tell her," Zelda says. She's loud; her voice carries and fills the whole playground, maybe all of Belling Bright can hear her. Usually when people talk to my father they flutter their eyelashes, they ask a hundred questions or they ask for advice or they ask to touch his hands, the ones that capture all that magic. Even when Dad's being difficult and people are seeing that, they are only ever quiet. They look away, they check in with my mother later to ask if everything's okay. They do not raise their voices or look him in the eye or do any of the things Zelda is doing right now.

I thought for a long time that meant that everyone respected my father. But right now, in the deserted playground, feeling the cold rush in, watching magical fireworks dot the sky and then fade, I know something else is true. They were afraid of him.

I know because I am afraid of him. I am watching his fingers itch at the tops of his legs. His throat bulges and his face looks like it is fighting something back.

"I suggest you return home," Dad says to Zelda, but it's obvious she's not about to go anywhere.

"Your old home," Zelda says.

"Rose. Let's go. This is a family matter."

"I agree," Zelda says. "And we're family."

The temperature plummets, and in an instant, Belling Bright is in winter again. I imagine snow might start falling any second. Usually I'm sad, when the magical weather of Ginger's party fades and we are left with the way things actually are. But today the cold feels good, like a reminder than there's really only so much magic can do.

Dad is quiet. He paces, and the pacing looks a lot like marching. His feet hit the ground like he's mad at it, and I know how Dad is when he's mad.

And I don't want Zelda to know.

I don't want anyone to know, really.

"We're not family anymore," Dad says at last.

"You get to just decide that?" Zelda asks. "That your family isn't your family anymore?"

"What does that mean?" I ask. "What are you guys talking about?"

"I told you to stay away from this girl," Dad says, turning all his awful energy toward me. "You should have respected that. You owed it to me to do *something* right."

I don't think he means to say it. Not like that, not in that tone of voice and with that little cover. He can't talk it away or pretend he meant something else. It's not like I didn't know how he felt about my failure. But we've been dancing around it and fighting against it and trying to picture it as something else entirely. Not anymore, I guess. Dad can only mean one thing: I owe him for how deeply I've disappointed him, and I have to try to be a better daughter now, since I'm not the daughter he thought I was.

"You know what I mean, Rose," Dad mumbles, but it's too late. "You're better than these people."

Maybe my dad has said a million untrue things over the years. He was wrong about things he seemed so sure about. But this untrue thing is the worst, the meanest, and the least true of all.

"I'll go," Zelda says, her voice deeper than it was a moment ago.

"You can't go," I say, flying my body toward her. I need

her here. I can't be alone with my dad right now. And I have a thousand questions that need answering. "You were saying—"

"I thought I wanted to—but this isn't what I wanted. We were just fine. Without all of this. Without all of you." I'd think maybe I should be the one crying, but it's Zelda's eyes that are watering, it's her chest that's shaking. She turns to my father. She isn't yelling at him anymore. The yelling was better; it meant she had hope. Now she's giving up, and I don't even know what she's giving up on. "My dad was right about you," Zelda says to my father, who won't look at her. "Just because you're his brother doesn't mean you're anything like him."

My heart loses itself for a second that could be an hour. "His brother?" I say, but I don't think it comes out as words so much as sounds and disbelief.

Zelda turns to me, finally. She's still crying. It's not a hard, heavy thing; it's not the way I've cried over Ginger and Maddy. The tears are fast but her breathing is slow. "You weren't the only one who was told to stay away," she says. "I thought—when you showed up I thought you knew we were cousins and you were ready to— But I don't want this. I don't want the way you all do things. I don't know what you're meant for. Magic or something else. But you're not meant for me."

Zelda is the same age as me. She looks a little like me,

from certain angles, I guess. And we grew up a mile away from each other. But when Zelda speaks she could be one hundred years old and from the moon. She says things I've never heard anyone else say; she does things no other kid in Belling Bright does.

"Cousins?" I ask, because I am not Zelda with smooth words and certainty and tears that don't make any noise. My voice catches and panics and I squeak and stutter even though I'm only saying one word.

"Whatever that means," Zelda says, her back already to me, her legs already walking to the far end of the playground and then away. I notice her bare feet, again, and my father's. It steals my breath in a way that feet shouldn't be able to do: that you can be family without even knowing it, the things we all share by accident. I want to show Dad, too. *Look, she has bare feet, she's one of us, we belong to each other.* But I don't. Of course I don't.

"Zelda! Wait!" is all I can actually manage to say.

Her shoulders shudder—she's still crying—and then she's gone, her bare feet moving her far away from here and us and this. Then I'm crying, not because she's my cousin, but because she doesn't want to be anymore. Because of all the secrets and then because of every way I've messed up and then, finally, I'm crying because Dad's still pacing and the pacing feels too big for his body, and for the playground and for the moment. Still, I can't stop myself from asking; I can't seem to stop talking and make it all better.

"Was that true? Is Zelda's dad—" I ask even though I know I shouldn't.

"You're meant for magic," Dad says.

"Okay, but is Zelda my—"

"You caught that jar."

"*Okay*, but do I have a—"

"You're my Little Luck. You are. You just are. That's what matters." Dad moves toward me, and I don't want him to touch me. So he doesn't, and we simply stand still and it's just me and my dad and the stories he's been telling me my whole life that aren't true, the things he wants me to be that I'm not, and the person everyone thinks he is that he's never actually been.

After a long while, we walk home in silence through the woods, maybe because it's a place we both like to be. Dad looks very intently at certain patches of dirt, certain flowers and trees. They must be the ones he made from his jars over the years. I imagine he has maps of his magic in his head, all the places he's opened jars and whispered things into being. I bet he checks on them from time to time, to see if they're still here, if the magic was as strong as he'd hoped.

"I think I've earned your trust," Dad says, stopping before we're all the way home. He doesn't like to walk and talk at the same time, so he turns to me and digs his heels into the ground.

"I think you've broken my trust," I mumble. I'd like to keep walking, but I don't want Dad yelling about anything else before the day is done.

"All I want is the best for my family and for Belling Bright and for the world, and that's it, Rose. That's all I'm trying to do. You understand, don't you?"

"I guess," I say.

"I'm not perfect," he says. "But I try so hard to make things right. And beautiful. And good. For you. For everyone." His eyes are teary. He wipes at them, and my heart breaks. I don't want to cry. And I see how hard he tries. I do. I see all the things he's done for all of us. "Do you understand?" he asks again, his voice cotton-soft and small.

"Sometimes," I say.

"I try to protect you. To make sure you have the best life."

I nod, and I understand and don't understand in the same uncomfortable moment. He watches me.

"I'm going to walk ahead," he says at last. "We both need time to think. I can see that. But Rose, remember all the good things in our life. Look around at all this magic, all this wonder, then tell me if you think it's fake. If I should have done everything differently. This is the world I helped build for us. For you. Think about that." I want to agree with everything he's saying because he looks so gentle and sad and Dad-like saying it. So I nod. And nod. And hug him. Because he looks like he needs a hug and he's my dad and I need a hug too.

But when he's walked ahead, I am mad again. And sad. And scared.

I look at the things he wants me to look at. There is so much beauty: heart-shaped trees and leaves that look like stars, flowers that are taller than me and trees that are tinier. Plants that sing and hum and feel like velvet and silk and clouds. Pink steam rises out of one blossom; a minuscule waterfall slides from the slope of another. He's right. I'm lucky to grow up here, in all of this. I'm lucky he helped make this place.

But if I'm so lucky, why am I also hurting? If this is all so right, why does it also feel kind of wrong?

I lean against a tree. I choose one of the large ones, built by our magical ancestors from ancient jars of magic. The bark is tough and scratches my skin. It's the kind of tree that has always been here and will always be here. It's the kind of tree I can trust and depend on and believe in.

Except, in a flash it isn't. With my full weight against it, in an instant so fast even my father couldn't possibly capture it in a jar, the whole tree vanishes. *Poof*, like it was never there at all. I topple to the ground and look around like maybe the tree is hiding, somehow, but of course it isn't. It's gone. The way all magic is eventually gone, the promise that none of it is forever, even if some of it is for a very, very long time.

Even the things that are the most certain, the most stable, can be gone in a flash, like they were never really there at all. My back and elbows and wrists hurt as I lie here, in the place where the tree used to be, in the place where magic once was but finally, at last, and with no warning at all, where magic finally wore itself out.

Thirty-three

A Story About Fishing That I Guess Was Actually
a Story About Something Else Entirely

Before I learned to catch fireflies I learned how to catch butterflies. And before butterflies, I learned how to catch frogs. And before frogs, it was fish.

There's a pond on the edge of Belling Bright, and that's where Dad took me to learn.

"It takes patience," he said. "You could use some patience. Patience will serve you well, Little Luck."

"But don't we have to be quick, when we're capturing magic?" I asked.

"We sure do."

"But also be patient?"

"We have to be a lot of things at once," Dad said. He smiled. He liked the challenge. He liked that not everyone could be both patient and quick. And I liked that too. Ginger's family would probably just let her be whoever she was. My dad wanted me to be more than that. I had to be things that made no sense together. Impossible things.

I wanted to be impossible. Impossibly lucky and impossibly special and impossibly magical. Like my father.

So I sat with Dad on the edge of the pond, my feet in the water, my shoulders burning in the sun, and I tried to be patient. For Dad, patient meant quiet. Quiet was hard for me. It made my throat hurt and my ears ring and it made my insides buzz with everything that was going unsaid.

Dad liked things going unsaid.

He splish-splashed his feet in the water every so often and hummed half tunes, but mostly stayed in silence. My mind was busy. I was wondering how long we would have to stay and how many fish were in the water, and what colors and shapes and sizes they were. I was thinking about Lyle back home and the sad face he'd made when he heard Dad was taking me, and only me, fishing. I was thinking about Mom looking worried, asking Dad if he was okay, reminding him to not get too upset with how the fishing went. *That* upset him, and his lips pursed in a funny, awful way. I was thinking about Evan Dell and the joke he made to me about how geography and geometry were kind of the same thing because they were both about the shapes of things. I thought about how I had laughed and accidentally snorted and tried to pretend it was a cough, but I was pretty sure he knew it was a snort. And Evan Dell said it wasn't a joke, it was a deep observation, and I felt like I'd messed everything up.

I was trying to think about fish.

It didn't go well. I hoped he didn't notice how not-well it was going.

"Oh!" Dad said, breaking the silence, interrupting his waiting and my not-waiting, and I looked to the water, assuming I would see a fish flapping its tail or the fishing rod bending from its weight. But the water was still and the line was steady and there wasn't so much as a tadpole swimming by.

I looked at Dad, to see where he was looking, and it wasn't at the water. He was looking *across* the water.

The pond was a small one. You could talk to someone on the other side without even raising your voice. So it wasn't hard to see the person Dad was looking at, the only other person at the pond. Dad had said the pond was a secret, so I'd thought it was a secret no one else knew existed.

"Someone's at our pond," I whispered. Even with a whisper, it was possible the person on the other side could hear me. But I didn't care.

"Don't get like that, Rose," Dad said, but I didn't think I was getting like anything. Sometimes it was hard to know what Dad's rules were and what I was allowed to say and do. It's not easy, following rules that no one's actually told you.

Calling the pond ours seemed safe, since it was something I'd heard from Dad's own mouth. But I guess it wasn't safe, because Dad's hand grabbed my arm, near the elbow, and squeezed. Sometimes Dad squeezed there a little harder than he needed to. Sometimes I could still feel the squeeze an hour later, or three. Sometimes the beginnings of tears appeared in the corners of my eyes and I had to wipe them away because it was silly and weak and not very Anders-like to cry because of an elbow squeeze.

Still, my eyes filled and I had to blink extra hard to get rid of the evidence. I knew how to do it because I had seen Mom do it. Blink, blink, blink, blink, breathe. Smile. Then, if needed, smile bigger.

Other rules no one told me but I needed to know about, I guess.

"We should go home," Dad said. We'd barely been at the pond two hours, and I'd thought fishing would be an all-day thing, sunup to sundown.

"We didn't catch anything," I said, even though the bruise by my elbow told me to shut up.

"We'll come back another day," Dad said.

"Wendell!" the man across the pond called. His voice was full and sweet, like Dad's but lighter. The kind of voice that sounds like a warm place you want to go in the winter, a voice that has been warmed up by a fire and a mug of cocoa.

Dad didn't respond. He was busy packing up worms and hooks and sandwiches.

"Wendell! It's me!" the man called.

"Dad?" I asked.

"Wendell, I know you can hear me. It's time we talked. It's time I met your kids and you met mine and we put this all—"

Dad didn't turn around. His back was to the man. I watched for his shoulders to wince or his head to turn or even for his foot to tap or his hands to lose their grip on the rod. But he moved as if there was no voice calling his name, as if the pond were an ocean and he wouldn't be able to hear a person across the water.

"Rose," the voice said, and I startled, hearing my own name. "I'm your—"

"That's enough," Dad bellowed, and he marched away, and I had no choice but to follow him. The way he stomped, the loudness of his words, made that clear.

Still, I let myself take one last look across the pond. The man was tall and skinny. He had a stubbly chin and blue eyes and a straight nose that looked like my father's. I let myself wave. I didn't really know why I was doing it, except that he'd said my name like he'd been wanting to say it his whole life.

He waved back, the man who looked familiar but not.

His hands were my father's hands. Large and slender-fingered. The wave was slow. His face was sad.

Back at the car, Dad's face was angry. His fingers were fast, tapping on the steering wheel, itching to do something else.

"Who was—" I started. I knew not to ask, but I asked anyway.

"No one," Dad said.

"He knew my name."

Dad didn't reply.

"He knew our secret pond."

Dad didn't reply.

"Dad?"

"Rose. There's nothing to talk about."

The road ahead stretched on long and empty all the way back to our house. Dad dropped me off when we got there. He didn't tell me what to tell Mom or help me bring in the equipment. He drove off without a word, when I'd barely even closed the door behind me.

"There was a man—" I started to tell Mom, but she shook her head like she didn't need to hear any more.

"Your father's under a lot of pressure," she said. I nodded, and Mom let me open a jar of magic that helped with sleeping and I took a nap so long it turned the day to night. When I woke Dad was home and dinner was set and no one was talking about the man across the pond or the fishing trip that wasn't or where Dad had driven off to.

Or the way my arm pounded and how I knew, better than I knew almost anything else, to pretend that it didn't.

Thirty-four

"I'm still mad at you," Zelda says. "I'm still confused, too. But Mom says family is forever, and anyway, I want to see it. I think I need to see it, to understand everything." She is on my front lawn moments after Mom and Dad and Lyle have gone off to Lyle's basketball game a few towns away. I wasn't invited. *You'll cause a commotion*, Mom said. *You can stay home and practice*, Dad said. *If you're there, no one will care about anything else*, Lyle said. He still seemed almost jealous of me, which was impossible because everything around me was falling apart.

"See what?" I ask Zelda. She must have known about the basketball game, somehow. She must have been hiding behind a bush, waiting for my parents to leave so that she could see me. I didn't know how badly I wanted her to be there. I thought I'd ruined everything. I want to throw myself into hugging her or telling her I'm sorry a hundred times, but I get the feeling she doesn't want that right now.

"I've never seen magic," Zelda says. "I want to see it."

"You just saw magic yesterday," I say. "You saw all kinds of magic."

"I want to see a jar of it," Zelda says.

"It's not very interesting," I say. "I can show you my dad's, I guess. Those are more—"

"I want to see yours."

I nod. Zelda lingers outside, though, like she has to take her time looking at our house. I try to see it through her eyes. It's enormous, compared to where she lives. It's too big, probably, and too shiny—Dad chose a silvery color for the outside and a shimmery pink for the shutters and a deep reddish-purple for the doors. It isn't so unusual for Belling Bright, but compared to where Zelda lives it's really something.

She probably wouldn't mind exploring the whole house, but I know my dad would freak out, and I'm too scared to let her go anywhere but my bedroom. He'd be mad enough about just that.

"Huh. It doesn't look like you," Zelda says when we get there, taking in my bedroom for the first time.

My room is bare-walled and blue-curtained. My dad

told me blue is a good color for attracting magic, and I believed him. He said bare walls left space for me to think my own thoughts, and he said that too many blankets on my bed would make me unable to handle the cold and discomfort of New Year's Day. I believed it all, and now my whole room is exactly the way he wanted it.

"My dad kind of . . ." I trail off because I don't know how to say the truth of it.

"Your dad's in charge of a lot of stuff," Zelda says. It's not a question.

"It's hard to explain."

"Well. It's easy to understand."

Sometimes I think Zelda might not be twelve like me, but might actually be like, seventy-five or something. At least, I think that's how many years it must take to sound so sure of everything, to shrug like she does, to say things that might be questions but have them be statements instead.

I pull my one jar from the shelf in my closet. I'm careful with it. I have known my whole life how to handle a jar of magic. Always use both hands. Always move slowly. Always watch your feet. Only take one slow step at a time. Do not let yourself forget, ever, what you are holding.

Zelda watches me watching the magic. She peers into the jar. I wonder if it looks different to her than it does to me.

"Can I touch it?" she asks.

"The jar?" I say. I don't want to hand it over. I hold it more closely to my chest.

"No, the magic," she says. "I want to know what it feels like."

I hold the jar closer still. This was a bad idea. Zelda is a bad idea. Letting her into my house, bringing her to the party, talking to her about magic, ignoring my father's rules again and again—all bad, bad ideas. I've trusted my dad my whole life; why did I stop now, when everything is the most delicate?

Zelda is reaching for the jar like she doesn't have any idea what could happen if it fell and broke, but I can't risk it; it was stupid to ever think I could. My heart beats out that she's my cousin, but the rest of me is practically screaming that I have to do what Dad wants, that that's the only way things don't fall apart, and things are so, so close to falling apart.

"You can't touch it," I say, a little more loudly than I intended. "I can't open this jar. This is all I have. If anything happened to it I'd be totally without any magic, which would be even worse than things are right now, which is basically impossible because things are terrible right now. This isn't—it's not some joke. It's not some fun thing to play with. It's magic. It's everything. And you don't get it. You don't get it, Zelda, you don't—you're not—"

There's a tiny collapse in Zelda's face. Not as big as what

happened at the playground last night, but unmissable anyway. "I'm not meant for it," Zelda says.

It's the truth, of course. And it's not something she hasn't said before. But this time it sounds different.

"You're not meant for it," I repeat, and I turn my back to her to return the jar to the closet. She thinks I'm protecting the jar, or myself, and I guess I am, but I'm protecting her too. She's Not Meant for Magic. And she's not meant for Wendell Anders, not even if she's his niece. No one's meant for this. But especially not Zelda, and I can't protect me and I'm not great at protecting Lyle or Mom, but I *can* protect her.

I hide the jar even farther back in the closet than it was before, behind my second-grade field day trophies and the box of handprint art I made when I was little. I wonder if Zelda made handprint art when she was little. I wish we could have done it together.

My wrist aches and I know it's about to start raining, so Zelda will have to leave soon, and my heart drops. I don't want her to leave, I realize. We've missed so much together, and we don't understand everything about each other, but maybe we could understand some very important things, if we really tried. Maybe I can tell Zelda everything I'm thinking about and all the things that don't make sense anymore and all the things that feel scary and all the secrets I have been hanging on to about what it's like to live in this magical house in Belling Bright with the most magical man in the world.

After all, I'm not Little Luck anymore. And my father isn't here. And I have a cousin. And I don't need this one jar, not really, not anymore, and I'm ready for something else.

So I turn around and step out of the closet to tell Zelda all of it, every last bit of what it is to be Little Luck, to be meant for magic, to have one jar of magic when you were supposed to have dozens, and how it's bad but also good but also terrifying.

But Zelda's already gone.

Thirty-five

It's just regular rain. It comes down at a regular pace the next day before school. It's loud, and it wakes me up, and I guess woke Lyle up too, because when I wander downstairs he's there. We were up together part of the night, as I told him about Zelda being our cousin and us having an uncle. He didn't say much but he nodded a lot. It takes Lyle a long time to figure out how he feels about something. I look at his face now. He's still trying to figure it out, I think. Maybe the rain will help.

It's the sort of rain Lyle and I used to like to play in. We'd put on boots but no raincoats because we liked the way our shirts felt when they were wet and heavy and clinging to us. There was something about being one person outside—wild and unworried—and another person inside—good and responsible—that felt delicious.

I wonder how Zelda feels about rain.

And I wonder if she is the same person out in the rain as she is inside. Probably she is. Probably Zelda doesn't care about rain like I do, because she can always just be Zelda—wet, dry, wild, quiet.

"Wanna go out in it?" I ask Lyle over oranges and toast at the breakfast table. "We have a little time before school."

"In the rain?" he asks.

"Just for a little," I say. "Like we used to." There's a list of things we used to do and used to be. We used to go for picnics. We used to laugh at old movies. We used to help Dad open jars of magic. We used to not worry about Mom. We used to think our family was perfect.

"I have plans," Lyle says. He looks out the window, though, like maybe he's thinking about it. Then he shakes his head.

"To do what?" I ask. No one has plans before school starts. It's not even possible.

"Nothing."

"You have plans to do nothing?"

"I guess."

"Magic," I say.

"Yeah." He says the word like it's an apology. He shouldn't have to apologize. I never apologized for all the time Dad spent teaching me about magic, all the time he spent pretty much ignoring Lyle. I never apologized for being the magical one, so he shouldn't either.

"It's fine," I say, but it's not really. "What are you using it for?"

Lyle shakes his head.

"Just tell me," I say.

Lyle sighs. "Come on, Rose," he says. "Eat your orange."

"Why aren't you telling me?"

He rubs his face. He's doing all the Lyle things he does, all in a row. "We're meeting early at school. We're going to try for a rainbow," he says. His shoulders fall and his head dips and even his voice drops down, down, down.

"Oh."

We stand there, Lyle and I, remembering the story of the rainbow that Dad told us a few years ago but also in another lifetime. We had talked about it from time to time over the years. When Lyle got his first magic, he made me a tiny rainbow charm on a bracelet. It wasn't his best magic, so the bracelet was too tight and turned my skin green, but it was a promise that I kept in the top drawer of my bedside table until the magic wore off and it vanished. It was a promise that one day we'd make a rainbow just like Dad's.

"I thought—" I start.

"Mom's been sad," Lyle says, before I can finish what he knows is coming. "I saw her crying. So I thought maybe a rainbow— I'd rather do it with you. You know that. But—"

"But I don't have any magic," I say.

"It's just a rainbow," Lyle says. "It's just something to try."

And I nod, like it's fine. But it's not fine and it's not nothing and it was supposed to be mine. The rainbow. The jars. The magic.

Thirty-six

By the time I get to school, it's there. The rainbow. And it's all anyone can talk about. We talk about it in math and in science, and in art class we all draw rainbows, but they don't look as good as what's in the sky. The rainbow Lyle and his friends made is blindingly bright and has a little sparkle to it. It's so beautiful I bet even Zelda and her family like it.

Or maybe they don't. Maybe even the most beautiful rainbow is ugly to them, if it's magical. Maybe Zelda's dad was there the day my dad made his rainbow. I wonder if he liked it then. If he noticed his mom crying. If he knew why she was so upset. If he was jealous of how beautiful he'd made the world, for that moment.

I know a little about being jealous. I am jealous of Lyle's rainbow and also of Ginger and Maddy, sitting in the cafeteria, whispering. They're at our old table and I'm at a table by myself, the one by the trash can that no one ever sits at because it smells like old food and gets splattered with mashed potatoes and refried beans when people throw their lunches away.

Every so often, someone magics it clean and sparkly and smelling like lemons. But it just gets dirty again, because even magic can't fix everything.

I try to think of what I would have done, if I had more than one jar of magic. Given myself an extra Saturday. Grown an extra inch. Tried to understand complicated math. Gotten better at drawing faces.

I guess that would be nice. But there would still be so many other things I couldn't fix. And even the things I could would be temporary and flimsy and, like Zelda's family—who apparently are my family—says, fake.

Maybe, I think, with an uneasy leap of my heart, I never really believed in magic at all.

"Weirdo," Layla says, interrupting my thoughts, which must have been written on my face, because she sees how I'm thinking weird things that no one else is ever thinking.

"You wanna draw a picture of me?" Westin asks, making poses at the table next to mine like he's some model.

"No wonder you didn't get any magic," Brent says.

"You're not meant for it." Brent didn't used to be mean. When we were six he taught me how to tie my shoes. When we were nine he stayed with me and held my hand after I took a big fall off my bike. But all that niceness seems to be gone. I guess you don't need to be nice, if you're magical.

"My mom told me that boy-crazy girls don't catch magic," Maddy says. She shrugs.

"I'm not boy-crazy," I say. "And that's a lie anyway."

"Only boy-crazy girls would draw pictures like that," Maddy says with another pointed shrug. Maddy takes her time tilting her head to the side and smiling. Brent and Westin laugh like weasels and Layla has a nervous giggle and more kids gather around to listen to Maddy tell me who I am, even though she has no idea. "You weren't ever serious about magic," she goes on. "You thought you could just get whatever you wanted by being Rose Alice Anders. You probably thought you'd get Evan Dell, too. But you were wrong, because you're some boy-crazy, silly, unpracticed, Not-Meant-for-Magic failure."

Eyebrows raise. Mouths open. But no one defends me.

Not Ginger.

Not even me.

But I don't run away from the moment. I stay. And the staying feels okay. This is my school. This is my town. I'm not Little Luck, but I *am* still Rose Alice Anders, and I don't know what I'm meant for, exactly, but I'm not meant for *this*.

"You won," I say to Maddy, because she did. She has all the magic and she has Ginger and she has extra-long hair with pink streaks in it and she has a dozen new outfits and she's going to get great grades and not have anyone thinking she's obsessed with Evan Dell.

I look at Ginger. She's been so quiet I could forget she's here. Except I can't, because some part of me is still waiting for her to be my old best friend.

Maybe magic does some really beautiful things. But it turns out it also breaks people apart. Ginger over there and me over here. Zelda on one edge of town and me on the other. My whole family in one house but also sometimes in our own universes.

I don't like it. And I don't think I need it. I take a big breath.

"Can I have my drawing back?" I ask. I make sure my back is straight when I say it. I make sure everyone can hear me.

Ginger's eyebrows raise right off her head.

"You know," I say. "The drawing. Of Evan Dell. Can I have it back? It's a really good drawing. That's why everyone knows it's him, right?"

"Right," Ginger says. She blushes, which is funny because I'm the one who should be embarrassed. "Um, Evan? Do you have that picture?" Evan Dell is sitting at the table next to Ginger's, and he shakes his head like he wants everyone to forget he's there, which is exactly what I've been doing, and it's weird, how Evan Dell and I have nothing in common but we somehow both want to disappear right now. Maybe Ginger does too. Maybe even Maddy and Layla and Brent want to be invisible sometimes. Maybe we're all hoping for jars of magic that can hide us when we're uncomfortable, can give us an escape from the moments that feel sticky and awkward and like they're going to last forever.

But the moments don't last forever. Not even this one. So if we can be a little patient and a little brave, we don't really need the magic at all.

"I don't have it with me," Evan Dell mumbles, and I have no idea if it's true or he wants it to be true, and it doesn't really matter, because I said what I needed to say and I'm not the one who wants to hide anymore.

"Well, whenever you think of it, get it back to me, okay?" I smile the biggest, brightest smile I have. I love that it is not magical at all. That it's just mine—the smile, the way I was brave, this moment where I am figuring out who Rose Alice Anders even is.

"Uh, okay," Evan Dell says.

"Cool, thanks," I say. And I don't walk out of the cafeteria. I stay at my trash can table and finish my lunch. I even go back for seconds.

Thirty-seven

A Story About When I Was the Mean One

When Maddy came to school two years ago, she said too much. She said too much and she wore clothes that were big and small in all the wrong places and she had this way of raising her hand and waving it around when the teacher clearly didn't want to call on her.

Ginger and I would smirk when she did it. We'd pass notes back and forth, commenting on different items of clothing. Her orange T-shirt. Her ankle-length brown skirt with big white buttons. Her beaded flip-flops.

I wonder if Ginger remembers it as well as I do.

I wonder if it makes her heart twist up, knowing how mean we were.

Maddy never caught us making fun of her. She kept trying and trying to be our friend, and finally she invited us over to her pool at the end of the school year. It was at least a hundred degrees out, and we didn't know anyone with a pool, because pool magic was usually pretty unstable, so pools never lasted long.

When we got to Maddy's that hot, hot day we threw on matching bathing suits—blue with red stars—and dove in at the same time. I think we wanted the water to splash Maddy's face. I think we wanted her to feel left out even at her own house.

Maddy didn't dive in. She sat on the edge of the pool with her legs kicking the water's surface. She watched me and Ginger do a dozen handstand contests. It took over an hour for us to say much to Maddy, and by that time she was biting her lip and staring at the sun like she was trying not to cry.

I didn't want to make someone cry. Not Maddy. Not anyone. Dad said that we couldn't solve every sad feeling with magic, and to not let people pressure me to help them and to worry about myself first. But this didn't have anything to do with magic, and this was a problem I could solve, and Dad's advice sometimes sounded weird when he wasn't right in front of me, when I was out in the world just trying to be a person.

"You don't like to swim?" I asked.

"I love to swim," Maddy said.

"You just don't want to do it today?" I asked.

Maddy's legs kicked the water faster. She dipped her fingertips in too. Swirled the water around. "I wasn't sure if you wanted me to," she said.

"It's your pool," Ginger said. She swam to the edge, where Maddy's feet were. I did too.

"I know, but it didn't— I wanted you guys to feel— I wasn't sure if I was really supposed to even be here."

"At your own house?" I asked.

Maddy scrunched up her face. All her features smushed together like they were on some sort of life raft and needed to stay as close as possible so as not to drown.

"Tell me what to do," Maddy said through that funny look on her face.

"What to do about what?" I asked.

"What to do to make you like me," Maddy said.

"We like you," I said, but even I heard how false it sounded. "But we don't know you that well. And also, like, we aren't really trying to find more friends."

"Rose!" Ginger said, like it wasn't the truest thing I'd ever said.

"What? We aren't!"

"Rose is rude sometimes," Ginger said, but she didn't correct me.

"I've never heard Rose be rude to anyone else," Maddy said. "Just me."

None of us said anything for a minute.

"I guess what she said is true," Ginger said at last. She was shivering. It's weird, how you're totally fine when you're in the water but then you stick your shoulders out for a minute and you're suddenly freezing. I could tell she wanted to dive back in but also wanted to be nice but also wondered why I wasn't fixing what I'd said. "It doesn't have to do with you, though. It's just been me and Rose for so long. For our whole lives. We don't think about making friends. Because we have each other."

"If we had a third best friend," I said, in one last attempt to fix things, "I'm sure it would be you."

Mom used to tell me to quit while I was ahead, but when Dad overheard her saying that to me he got mad. *That kind of advice is for other types of people*, Dad had said. *Not Little Luck here. She doesn't ever have to quit. You hear me, Luck? Don't ever quit. Not when you're ahead. Not when you're behind. Not ever.*

I guess that's why I said what I said. Maybe what Ginger had said would have been enough. Maybe it would have fixed everything. I don't know. But I felt like there was more to say, and that I was the person to say it, so I did. Dad had

257

so many rules, and I tried my best to follow them all, and I didn't worry too much about anything but following those rules so he'd be happy with me.

And this time, as soon as the words left my mouth, Ginger started bobbing in the water again and Maddy jumped in, her face all flushed and smiley like I'd given her the best news ever, even though I didn't really think I'd given her any news at all.

We played a few rounds of Marco Polo and did a few more handstand contests, and then we all got chilly and tired and wrinkly, so we lifted ourselves out of the pool and into the pool chairs, and it was about time to leave when Maddy gave a big sigh.

"I'm so glad you have room for me," she said. "I'm so glad we can all be best friends now."

It wasn't what we'd told her. Not at all. Not at *all*. But she sounded so sure and so happy that it wasn't possible to correct her.

Ginger and I sort of slumped ourselves home and we ate dinner outside on my front lawn like Mom always let us do when Dad wasn't around. Mom hated cooking, so on her nights we got cheese and crackers and carrot sticks and as many peaches and pears as we wanted and we'd lay it all out on a blanket on the lawn and graze for hours, for as long as we were hungry and sometimes after.

We stayed outside for so long that Mom fell asleep on

the couch and forgot about us and Dad found us out there and joined us, picking at the fruit and the crackers.

We tried to tell him what had happened and why we felt so uneasy.

"You have to worry about who you surround yourself with, Rose," he said. "And you have to help her, Ginger."

"Oh," Ginger said. I didn't say anything.

"This Maddy sounds like a girl who won't capture much magic at all. I'd stay away from her," Dad said. "Girls like that aren't anything like you. They aren't worth the trouble."

We nodded. We always nodded at Dad and the things he said, which sounded like fact but maybe, maybe weren't so true at all.

Thirty-eight

Today, when I get to Zelda's house, I hide behind a tree across the street, like I'm some spy.

I'm flushed from all my truth telling and the way it feels to maybe just be Not Meant for Magic instead of trying so hard to be something else. But I'm still too scared to approach Zelda and her family.

My family.

I can't stop looking at Zelda's dad. I want to know if we have the same ears and if he pronounces words like *bureau* and *mirror* and *garage* the way I do. If there's some unexpected thing we share, like Zelda and my father and their always-bare feet.

But also. I want to know if he is ever meaner than you

expect him to be, if he says and does things he has to apologize for later.

Right now, though, he's outside with Zelda and his other daughter, Lucy, and the three of them are doing what Zelda loves to do most of all. They're making dandelion crowns. Zelda's is enormous, more of a belt or a very long necklace than a crown. And her sister is making a bunch of super-small ones—maybe rings? But it's her father I can't take my eyes from. His fingers know their way around a flower crown the same way Zelda's do. He squints at it, brings it close to his face, and smiles at his work. He adds grass to the dandelions, braiding strands in to make it thicker and sturdier. He puts it on his head to try it on, then takes it off to work on it some more. He leans over to Zelda and asks her to look at some part of it, and she fixes a knot for him. When she turns back to her own work, he smiles at her like she's done something truly spectacular.

They're all smiling and easy together. They have all the time in the world to braid dandelion and grass into jewelry, all the time in the world to be right here, in this exact moment.

I have never been so still with my father. I have never seen him make a flower crown or sit in the grass and just be. He has not smiled at me in that slow, easy way. He has grinned at the way I catch a firefly in my palms or how I answer questions from reporters. He has beamed when people talk about me, call me Little Luck, tell him how special I am, how special I am going to be.

But we haven't sat in the grass and done not much at all.

Zelda's mother comes outside and kisses each of their heads. She looks at the crowns, sniffs the flowers, says something that sounds sweet and silly from here, and goes back inside.

It is all so simple, the way they are together. Zelda leans her head on her dad's shoulder, and I think my heart breaks, or at least some important part of it tears a little.

I try to imagine my family sitting with them. It shouldn't be hard to see. Our feet are the same shape, we have the same hair texture—almost curly but not quite, the same gaps in our teeth. I think our hands braid grass the same way, even.

Still, they don't belong to me.

It feels like watching Ginger and Maddy and their magic. Zelda with her father is a thing I thought I had but don't, a life someone sort of promised me but was never actually mine.

"You and your dad are so close!" Ginger would always say with starry eyes and a sort of sigh once her dad died. And I thought that was true, but the closeness had something else attached to it—the promise of being like him, of succeeding, of being someone great.

He only ever told me one way to be great.

But maybe this is something great too. Maybe there is something else that matters, something that isn't magic but is special all the same.

Maybe if you aren't meant for magic, that only means you are meant for something else. And maybe that something else might be nice, too.

Thirty-nine

*A Story About the Weather
and Also Magic and Also My Father
and Also How They Don't All Fit Together So Well After All*

We watched Dad make a storm once.

It was the middle of the summer and it had been so dry that the grass was brown and trees looked thirsty and the flowers were drying out and we were all taking three-minute showers every other day to conserve water.

"Weather is a powerful kind of magic," Dad said, bringing out three jars—one a cloudy gray, one a small pool of water, one that looked totally empty but felt cool when you touched it. "Don't play with it, okay? Don't play with any magic, but especially not weather."

I remember rolling my eyes and Ginger rolling hers

back because we would never use our magic for something like weather. Not when we could use it to make a great Halloween costume or permanently hot-pink fingernails or a tree house in the woods behind the school.

"We have stuff to do, Dad," I said.

"Really important stuff," Ginger said.

"Well, you can do your really important stuff later," Dad said. "Watch this. You won't regret it."

Dad liked to do magic in the backyard under the three maple trees that clustered in the middle of the lawn. Those maple trees never looked quite right. They were too close together to look like they were meant to be there. They were definitely made from magic. Not Dad's—someone from long ago, someone with powerful, long-lasting magic. But someday it would run out, and those trees wouldn't be there anymore.

We were used to huddling under them, Ginger and I, with Dad holding his jars up to the sunlight to check how much magic was left in each one, and what kind of magic each might be. Dad knows how to mix his magic up like potions, to make sure they do what he wants them to do. Most other people use each jar all at once, and all on its own. Dad has his own way with magic, sprinkling a dab of this one with a sprinkle of that.

That day was no different. He opened the smoky gray jar, the jar with the pool of water, the cold empty jar.

"We need a lot of rain," he said. "Use a watery magic for rain. Logical." He was talking to us but also to himself. "This magic looks foggy. If you use it for the wrong thing, you'll end up very unhappy, I'll tell you that much," he said to the gray jar. "I've seen people use foggy magic like this to help make food, and it tastes burnt. Magic is particular, girls. That's why you need to capture all different kinds. Okay? You're hearing me, right?"

We nodded. Somewhere in my bedroom and in Ginger's we kept notebooks of advice from my dad. Tonight we'd write down never to use foggy gray magic for food, that magic is particular, that we have to be careful.

Dad held the jar of foggy magic up to the jar with the little puddle inside. They stirred themselves up in the air, and he grabbed an empty jar to capture the new mixed-up magic. If anyone else were watching, they'd be amazed. I'd never seen anyone else do magic that way. I hoped and hoped I'd be able to do it someday.

"And cold magic—cold magic is very strong. Not everyone knows that. We don't need much." He held the cold jar to the jar with the new magical mix. A storm was brewing.

When the cold hit the rest of the mix, the whole thing got twirlier and swirlier and stranger. Inside the jar, it looked like a hurricane.

"That looks strong," I said.

"That looks scary," Ginger said.

"That's why we're careful," Dad said. "More than careful—patient. This isn't ready yet. This magic needs time to calm down."

We waited by baking cookies and watching a movie that Dad loved on the couch. We waited by playing Monopoly and making paper dolls with the scraps of fabric samples from Mom's newest decorating project.

Before dinner, Dad said the waiting was over. We went outside with him and his jar. What was inside was whirling and powerful.

"Don't release it," I said.

"Rose. It's to help the drought." Dad had a smile that sometimes made me nervous. A smile that looked like it had a secret.

"Then why make a whole storm?" I asked. "We just need a little rain."

"We don't have small magic in this family," Dad said. "We do things big or not at all. You remember that. That's how we got here. That's how we became us. We make big storms when a little one would do. You hear me, Rose?"

I said okay. But I was pretending. Maybe Ginger was just pretending, too. I said okay and she said okay and Dad released the magic, the whole swirling, dangerous mess of it.

It made trees fall. It flooded the streets. The town lost power.

But Dad didn't apologize. Not even when Mom asked him to.

Especially not when Mom asked him to.

The storm raged for a week. He didn't say he messed up. He didn't apologize. He didn't ask if maybe magic was sometimes all wrong. He didn't wonder if maybe he should have let things happen as they were supposed to, instead of as he wanted them to.

He let the storm rage.

Whenever it rains now, I get uneasy, trying to forget the way that magic is not actually always in our control. Trying to forget how Dad isn't always under control either.

Forty

When I get home, they are waiting for me. Lyle on the stairs. Mom and Dad in the living room. All of them cloudy-faced in spite of Lyle's rainbow, still pinned to the sky.

"Where were you?" Dad booms.

"Wendell," Mom says in a hushed tone. "Breathe, please."

"Trust me, I'm breathing! I need to know where my daughter was. You left school and should have come right home, and someone said they saw you walking out there, out to that house—"

"I wanted to see—" I start, but he doesn't let me finish.

"It's enough, Rose. You stay here. You practice for next year. You stop trying to make a show out of your failure."

"Rose. Lyle. We need a moment; can you two head upstairs to play?" Mom says.

I am twelve and Lyle is fifteen and we don't really play anymore, but we know how to leave a room. And we sort of know why we have to leave a room, too.

Lyle goes up the stairs and I follow and we sit right at the top, at the place where we can hear a little but not too much. Dad says something about how Mom loves places without magic and Mom says something about how Dad needs to accept me for who I am, and then Lyle covers up by starting a game of A is for Alice who uses Aromatic magic on her Apples, and I love him for it.

And I guess I was wrong. We do play, when we have to.

"B is for Benny, and she uses Bringing Together magic on Bears," I say.

"C is for Claude, and he uses Calculus Learning magic on . . . Cactuses," Lyle says. He can always make me smile.

"She needs to be working harder." Dad's voice gets a little louder when we are at "J is for Julia who uses Juggling magic on jaguars." "She needs to try. She's—with that girl! She's giving up. You can see it in her eyes. Tell me you can't see it in her eyes. That she's changed. That she isn't ours anymore."

"Wendell." Mom's voice is loud and final. "Rose choosing not to— Rose liking her cousin— That doesn't mean

Rose isn't our girl. She'll always be ours. But she's herself, too. And it's high time you and your brother started mending fences. Maybe he has a point. There are places where magic isn't so—"

"When we got married I told you what mattered to me, what I wanted for our family, who we are meant to be—"

"Maybe she's Not Meant for Magic," Mom says. It's quiet. Maybe I misheard her. But I feel Lyle stiffen next to me, and I know what she said.

And I know that it is a true thing that she said.

I start to stand, to tell her thank you, to say yes, that is it, that is the thing; I am Not Meant for Magic and I am happy to be Not Meant for Magic and I wonder if anyone is meant for magic or if magic really knows what's best at all.

It's going to be okay. The truth was there, it was said, it's out of her mouth, and I can just exist in it.

"Mom, Dad, I think—" I start.

But then there's a sound I don't recognize except I sort of do in a very faraway part of my brain or heart or, I don't know, my limbs. The sound is hot and hard and quick and then it's over except there's all the sounds after, which are mostly Mom's crying and the dropping of a dish she was maybe washing or putting away, and then Dad's voice saying *I'm sorry I'm sorry I didn't mean to I'm sorry I just hated what you said and I can't hear that kind of thing and you know*

I'm sorry and would never—

I reach for Lyle's hand, because I don't know what exactly I heard except I am absolutely positive about what I heard.

Then there's Mom's voice floating up and up and up, quieter than it's been, maybe quieter than it's ever been, but I'm straining so hard to hear anything but that awful sound that I can actually hear it.

"It's okay," she says, but it can't possibly be. "It's okay. I'm okay. It barely— You barely— It's okay."

Forty-one

Maybe it is five minutes. Or it might be five hours. Seconds. Maybe time stops existing after that sound, and what we know it means and what it has probably always meant.

They don't speak, but they leave. Mom first, her feet tiptoeing, and I know she's hoping we didn't hear and I know she also must understand that we did. Still, she doesn't look at the top of the staircase on her way out the door. That way, she can pretend we weren't there at all.

I can't see her whole face on the way out. Just her hand pressed against her cheek, like it can stop the hurt.

It cannot. I'm sure of that.

Dad leaves next, right after Mom, and I swear I can hear his heart beating from up here, but maybe that's Lyle's heart,

273

or mine, even. I don't know where they're going, except that I know I want to escape the house too. If we stay here, the things that happened are real.

We wait awhile. We don't speak except through the beat of Lyle's heart and the way my fingers tap on my thighs. Maybe if we don't move, everything will be okay. Maybe if we stay just like this, we'll be safe.

I wonder if we realize in the same moment that we were never safe. That magic never fixed anything. Because Lyle shifts his legs, turns his head my way at last.

"You're right," he says. He has to say it again, because his voice in the air after what we've heard doesn't make sense at first. I've forgotten words and language and everything except for how badly I want things to not be what they are.

"About what?" I ask.

"Magic," he says.

"I don't even know what I think about magic," I say. "There's nothing for me to be right about." Lyle shakes his head, though.

"Everyone thinks he's so magical and so special," Lyle says. It takes a great effort to say it. "And we have all these jars. And I thought the jars were hope. Like some promise that everything would always be great. That we could make things beautiful."

I know what he means. The jars crowding all the shelves, all the jars in the closets and on the windowsills and the very best ones on the mantel—they were all there to tell us that things would be wonderful, that we were wonderful, that our life was beautiful, that we were special, that whatever we wanted would be ours.

But here we are, with more magic than the rest of Belling Bright combined, and still the world is scary and our home is sad and we are hiding the things we don't want people to know about us. We are wanting things to be different than they are, but there's no magic that can do that. Not really.

"I don't want to stare at a jar of magic thinking it can make everything great anymore," Lyle says.

"Me neither." I don't know quite what it means to be saying this. Magic glints at us from every direction, every corner of our home. It floats in the jars, glows and sparkles and shimmers and stays. We are outnumbered by it. We are drowning in it.

And it didn't fix a single thing.

But maybe getting rid of it could fix something.

"I'm done with it," Lyle says, and he doesn't sound sure, but he sounds like he wants to be sure. "I'm done with magic."

"Do you trust me?" I ask.

"Yes." He is more certain of this. It is a fact that has always been true.

"Then I know what to do."

I get up off the steps. My legs aren't so steady, so Lyle has to help me. We hang on to each other for a second to get our balance. It comes. The steadiness. And with that we walk down the stairs, and I take the first jar off the mantel. It is pink. It glows. Maybe it is for love or wellness or the pink hair that Ginger and Maddy and Layla got for themselves.

I don't know.

I'll never know.

And I don't have time to think about it. We have a lot to do.

Forty-two

Zelda arrives with three suitcases, four backpacks, and her dad, who waits outside in his car. She is wearing a flower crown, and I want to be wearing one too; it feels like I need one, for this moment.

"You came," I say.

"You asked me to," she says.

"But you're mad at me."

Zelda shakes her head. She looks at the jars of magic we've taken off the shelves, extracted from the closets. They're on the ground, lined up the way Mom brings in bags of groceries that need to be put away. They look different here, like this. Casual. Unimportant.

"I told you before. Family is forever. I can be mad at

you and still want to help you," Zelda says. She's saying it all casual and unimportant too, but it feels huge to me. A sentence I'd never considered before.

"You can?" I ask.

"Mad isn't a forever thing. It's not even the most powerful thing. It's just a thing you feel sometimes, before you feel something else." Zelda adjusts the crown on her head. She shrugs.

I have a hundred questions about how it's possible to think of anger as just one more thing a person might feel, instead of the thing you should be most afraid of in the whole wide world. It doesn't feel true, but in the same breath, it also feels very true. Looking at not-angry Zelda makes it seem like it could be true.

It didn't last forever, her being mad at me. And it didn't make anything awful happen. It didn't make the world collapse. It didn't make Lyle and me hide out on the roof. It didn't make my mother cry.

"I don't know you very well," I say.

"Same," Zelda says.

"I don't know anyone but my dad super well sometimes," I say, which is closer to what I wanted to say. What I want to say is that Wendell Anders is so big in so many ways that it's hard to remember other people do things differently, have lived different lives, feel different things. Wendell Anders is so big he makes you believe in the exact way he sees the world.

He is so big, I still don't know exactly who I am, so I can't possibly know quite who Zelda is, but I'd like to. I'd really like to.

"It's easier without magic," Zelda says. And maybe she means getting to know people is easier without magic, but maybe she means everything is easier without it.

Maybe, in spite of everything, things will be easier without these jars.

I put one in Zelda's suitcase. Then three more. Six. A dozen. The suitcases fill up fast with the three of us working. Our backpacks fill up too. Our pockets are stuffed with small jars. We find tote bags and grocery bags and Mom's old purses.

We don't know when our parents are returning, so we move quickly and soundlessly. There will be more time to talk about what a magic-less life looks like, more days to wonder about anger and how it hangs on different people, and whether it's something to even be scared of.

Someday, we can all talk about Wendell Anders and whether he was ever the person he said he was and what magic means and why he got so much and why I captured almost nothing at all.

Sometime, maybe a long time from now, or maybe in

a day or two, which feels like a pretty long time from now anyway, we will figure out whether it was ever true, that you get the magic you deserve, the magic you are worthy of.

But not now.

Right now, we have to decide what to do with hundreds of jars of magic that maybe don't mean what we thought they did.

"We can just open them up," Zelda says. "Bring them to my house and release them all."

"Into the air?" Lyle asks. He is aghast. I am too, but I try not to show it so that I don't hurt Zelda's feelings.

"I guess," Zelda says. She sounds less sure, though. She's remembering how very little she knows about magic and what it can do. "It doesn't last forever, right? Magic?"

"Not forever, but it can last a long time, decades. Centuries," I say. "And opening those jars could cause—" I start, but I actually have no idea how the sentence ends. No one has ever opened up dozens of jars of magic at once, with no plan or thoughts on what they want the magic to be used for. "Well, I don't know what it would cause, but it would be bad," I finish.

Zelda nods.

"The lake," Lyle says.

"What lake?" I ask, because he can't possibly be saying what I think he's saying.

"TooBlue Lake," he says, and it almost makes me laugh.

"That's where the magic's from. So that's where it should go back to."

"We can't get there," I say.

"We're not allowed to go there," Zelda says.

"We're not allowed to steal Dad's magic either," Lyle says. "But here we are."

"Here we are," I say. "Zelda? Do you think your dad would drive us there? He wants to get rid of the magic, right?"

"I don't know if he wants to get rid of it exactly. . . ." Zelda says. "He wants—I don't know. He wants it not to matter. Or not to matter so much. Especially—well, especially to you, Rose."

"To me?" I hadn't thought Zelda's dad ever thought about me. I thought he wanted to stay far away from me and my magical family.

"That's all he's ever wanted," Zelda says. "For it to not matter if you're meant for magic or not. For you to be Rose, without all the worrying about jars. . . . For your father to—well, I guess for your dad to stop caring about being the magical Anders family and to just be, you know, a family."

"We're a family," Lyle says, but he doesn't say it with a lot of force. He doesn't say it like he believes it.

"Sometimes," I say, and I'm thinking of eating dinner outside in the summer, and celebrating Lyle's birthday at the movies. Going on a hike in the woods behind our house.

Having a sleepover in the living room when our bedrooms were getting painted and Mom was scared of the fumes and Dad said we should have just used magic and Mom said we couldn't use magic for everything, and Dad nodded just the littlest bit, and maybe he didn't totally agree but he didn't disagree and that was something, it was *something*, it was a small moment of being just a family. And in that small moment I remember wishing our nights were always that cozy and sweet and unmagical.

It was a long time ago. Maybe it was always. Maybe there has always been a big part of me wishing for less magic, not more.

And maybe that's why I'm Not Meant for Magic. Because I don't believe in it. Not really. Not the way Dad does.

"Are we really doing this?" I ask. We could put the jars back. Pretend Zelda was never here, put our backpacks and suitcases and bags back where they came from, stop thinking of ways to change the world we've always lived in.

But if we drive these jars of magic to TooBlue Lake, that's it: the world will never be the same, our family will never be the same, Belling Bright will never be the same.

I wouldn't mind everything changing, because for me everything already *has* changed. But for Lyle—he can't want that. He could still live a totally normal life with a totally normal amount of magic. He has all the same friends he had before New Year's Day, and he could keep going to their houses, playing their video games, coming up with ways to use their dwindling jars of magic until the next New Year's.

Except our dad would stay the way he's always been. The way we've tried to pretend away, or ignore away, or just stay very quiet and still about. Nothing changes, unless everything changes. Wendell Anders is a big force. Magic is a big force. So we have to do something even bigger to make it different.

"I'm sure," Lyle says, in spite of everything. "Maybe I'm Not Meant for Magic either."

"But you've always caught magic," I say.

"Maybe magic doesn't know what's best. If magic was perfect, if it always went to the right people—I don't think so much of it would have gone to our dad. And so little to you." Lyle speaks in a mumble; he doesn't quite look at me.

I wonder if he's thinking what I'm thinking—that people have always loved Wendell Anders for his big laugh and his big personality and his big, big magic. But they didn't really know him. And maybe magic didn't know him so well either.

"Nothing's perfect," Lyle says. "Not even magic."

"Especially not magic," Zelda says.

Forty-three

"Wait," Lyle says, before we take the last of the bags outside and into Zelda's dad's car. "Are we sure?"

"About what?" I ask. We are so far in, it feels way too late to be unsure about something, even if there's a nervous ache in my stomach and a whole unknown world opening up in front of us to feel unsure about.

"Maybe we shouldn't get rid of everything," he says.

"Isn't that the whole point?" I ask. My voice is rising, as if I'm angry, but all I really am is scared. I need Lyle to be certain, because if he's not, then I have to be, and I can't be.

"One jar is okay," Zelda says. Her voice is quiet in a way it's never been, and her eyes are wide and kind and telling me I can take a breath. So I do. I take a breath. And another.

"One jar?" I ask.

"Keep one jar. One jar to never use." Zelda smiles, and I can't remember when I smiled last, and it's weird, how you can get so used to being sad that being happy seems absurd, that even smiling seems like a little too much.

It's funny, how something hard can start to feel normal. How sadness can start to feel like okay-ness, how fear can feel like skin, a thing that you can't be separated from. It's funny, how easily the way things *are* can feel like the way things *have* to be.

"Why would we—" I start to ask at the same time as Lyle starts to sort through his bags, looking for something special. He likes the idea. I don't think I understand it.

"My dad has one," Zelda says. Another secret revealed. I hope it's the last one, but something tells me it's not, that the world is filled with secrets, and they will pop up from time to time and shake us up, and we won't have magic to set things right again.

"Your dad has a jar of magic?" I ask. "He's not meant for it, though."

"I just found out," Zelda says. "Just now. He showed it to me. It's pink. The jar is old. The top's on really tight. It's been in our house this whole time. Up in the attic. In a box with my old toys."

"But why?" I ask. The whole point of magic is to use it.

The whole point of jars is to count them up and have the most.

"He liked it," Zelda says with a shrug. "He said having a jar that you never use is beautiful. It's like trusting yourself and the world to have enough magic for you without the kind of magic you find at TooBlue Lake. He says every day he doesn't open that jar, even the hard days, is one more day that he believes in himself, one more day that he thinks he is enough."

There's a long silence.

Maybe Lyle is having a long rush of memories, just like me. Times that we've been sad and Dad's promised us we'll be able to fix it with magic. Times we've felt small or not smart or not pretty or not cool or, sometimes, *sometimes*, not loved. Not safe. And that we were promised we could change all of that with a jar of magic. The whole town, the whole world, was given that promise. That if there's some way you want to be better, some way you want the world to be better, you can have that, if you capture enough magic. If your magic is strong enough to last a good long while.

And all this time, Zelda's father has decided to *not* change things with magic. He's had it right there, and instead he's decided that he's enough. That their home at the edge of Belling Bright is enough. That his family is enough.

I thought being Not Meant for Magic meant you

weren't good enough for it. But maybe it means you choose to believe in something else, something bigger and better than magic. Maybe I only caught one jar of magic because my heart knew a hundred jars don't solve anything.

A hundred jars cause more problems than they solve.

Problems Lyle and Mom and I try so hard not to talk about.

Problems I was never very good at ignoring.

I look at Zelda. She's always been enough. Just like this. Just the way she is right this second, with tangled hair and knobby knees and some dirt under her fingernails and not doing anything very special, not doing anything worth mentioning, just standing here trying to help us. And I don't know, maybe that's the exceptional thing.

Or maybe there's no need to be exceptional when you can just *be*.

"We all keep one jar," I say, nodding. Lyle's already ahead of me; he's picked a good one. It's dark and shimmers a little like the night sky, and the magic inside moves like there's a tiny breeze behind the glass. I know the story of it—he caught it in the dark of night; he had a feeling there was magic in a certain patch of nighttime air and he swung his jar at it and closed it tight and he caught a kind of magic that isn't so easy to catch.

We pick out one of Dad's and one of Mom's—something that looks like rain for Dad, since he loves stormy magic, something that looks like sunlight for Mom, since it seems like that's something she'd like to look at. And then it's time for me to choose my jar, except I don't have an array of jars to choose from. I just have my one jar. It doesn't shimmer and shine or remind me of a wonderful moment. In fact, a few days ago, I would have liked to get rid of it entirely, for reminding me of all the ways I don't measure up, all the things I don't have that everyone else has.

But today it looks different. I mean, it looks the same, but I see it differently.

It's a plain jar and it has only the tiniest bit of magic inside and I didn't even catch that magic by myself.

And maybe I was meant for more than this one jar of magic; maybe Dad thinks I was promised something more special, some greater destiny.

But a promise isn't the same as the way things are, and the promise was dozens of shiny, fancy jars, but the reality is this one jar of almost-nothing. But this one jar of almost-nothing maybe means I don't need more, I don't have to have magic to make myself better. Maybe capturing only one jar of magic means I am enough, just like this.

Forty-four

Zelda's father's eyes are wide at the sight of all these jars of magic.

"He really— He got all of that, huh?" He looks sad, like something must have gone wrong for there to be so much magic in one place.

Lyle and I nod, and Zelda's father, our uncle, shakes his head. "No one should have that much," he says. "He still going out there to steal it?"

There's a break in the world turning. Or at least it feels that way.

"Steal?" Lyle asks. He feels it, too. The shift. It's not just the jars of magic that are all getting piled into the car.

It's that word. And how casually Bennett said it. Like we already knew.

"Well, one person can't catch so much at once," Bennett says, but more slowly, like he can tell he's shaking the world up for us too, like we're stuck in some snow globe that's never had snow. And now, all of a sudden, a blizzard's coming down. "There's not this much magic at once anywhere. Ever. Not even TooBlue Lake on New Year's Day." He looks at us to see if we had already known this. We did not. Not exactly. I move closer to Lyle.

"Our father catches more than a hundred jars every year," Lyle says. There's still a flush of pride there. It's hard to let it go.

"I'm sure he does," Bennett says. "But not all at once. He goes back throughout the year. He finds more on his own when no one else is around. When you're not really supposed to—"

"No," Lyle says. "That's not allowed."

Bennett hangs his head. "I haven't talked to your father in many years," he says carefully, "but that's what he used to do. It's what I did, a long time ago with him. When I thought magic was—when I thought I was meant for it. When I believed in it. When I believed in . . . well, in him."

I know it's true as soon as he says it. Not just because our uncle seems so steady and so quiet and so good. But also because I have been there. I have gone to TooBlue Lake with my father when it wasn't New Year's Day. I have seen how natural it was for him. I have seen him sniff the air, looking. I have seen the extra jars. I have seen, without seeing. I have known, without knowing.

"That's not fair," I say.

"Why would he do that?" Lyle asks.

"Your father—he thinks magic—we both for a long time thought magic could fix things. Big things."

"It can," Lyle says, but I am starting to know it cannot. Because it didn't fix the things that are the most wrong about us.

"We didn't have the best time growing up, your father and I." He looks at us in the rearview mirror. His eyes are exactly like Dad's but also completely different. When they look at us, they really see us. They aren't looking for more. They aren't assessing. They just *are*. "Families can be hard for all kinds of reasons," he says. "Ours was— We had a dad who wasn't very predictable. And sometimes that meant we got hurt."

I nod. I don't want him to say any more, because I know what it all means.

He doesn't say another word until we are at TooBlue Lake, and then he doesn't say anything there, either. We get out of the car and unload the suitcases and bags and backpacks and ourselves.

And even though he doesn't tell me what he's thinking, I know, from the way Zelda's dad looks at the tops of the trees and puts a hand on my shoulder, that his father was a lot like my father. And that he never thought he and his brother would turn out so different.

"Was your dad mean?" I ask our uncle Bennett. It's not quite the question I want to ask, but close enough.

"He didn't try to be," Uncle Bennett says.

"But he was anyway?" I ask. I know the answer. Uncle Bennett knows I know the answer.

Forty-five

We unpack the jars one by one and line them up on the shore. They glint and glimmer and shine. They are beautiful. They are a lifetime of work.

But they are my father telling me over and over that he got the most jars because he deserved them the most. And they are my father getting the most jars because he went out and stole them.

They are my father saying magic knows everything.

And they are me knowing, now, that magic can be just as swayed by a handsome man who loves scarves and bare feet and oatmeal-colored sweaters and has a big booming laugh and a perfect smile as anyone else.

Magic can be wrong.

We can be wrong.

Some days, the whole world can feel wrong.

But these jars on the shore are right. If only we can figure out what to do with all their magic.

"He's going to be so mad," Lyle says. He's flushed, because fear makes him turn red, and I'm scared too. At how Dad will feel. And also at Lyle using that word.

Mad.

We don't use that word to talk about Dad.

"It's okay," I say, knowing it also sort of isn't. "He—" I try to think of a way to smooth this out. I've been doing it my whole life, smoothing out the rough edges of Wendell Anders. Telling stories a little differently than the way they happened. Finding reasons for the things he does and says and is. Making it sound better, even to myself.

But I'm having trouble today.

"He's mad a lot, isn't he?" Zelda's dad asks.

Lyle freezes. I look harder at the lake, like maybe if I stare at it enough it will swallow me up and I won't have to answer. It's a question I have wanted to ask my whole life but also wanted to make sure I never, ever asked. *Does Dad get mad a lot? What's a lot? What's too much? What's normal?*

"What's normal?" I say here and now, finally, even though what I really want is to live at the bottom of TooBlue Lake and not out here anymore, where everyone can see me and wonder about me and judge me and worry about me.

"There's no normal," Zelda's dad says. "Or if there is, we're not it. But there's okay and not okay."

"What's not okay?" I ask.

"If you're scared of him," Zelda's dad says, "that's not okay."

"Oh," Lyle says.

"Even just sometimes?" I ask, which I guess is about the same as admitting I am sometimes scared of my dad, but it feels sort of like Zelda's dad knows that anyway, like that's kind of the whole point of us being here in the first place.

"You don't seem like someone who gets scared very easily," Zelda's dad says.

"She's not," Zelda says. Then she turns to me. "You're not."

We all watch the lake for a while. I think I can feel the magic under us, making the sand a little warmer or making the ground a little shaky. I think maybe I can even hear it too. A whisper, a shadow of a sound, a thing I've been hoping to hear my whole life, a thing I was promised.

But before I can enjoy the prettiness of it, or even just the there-ness of it, I hear my dad in my head telling me he knew I was special and then asking why I couldn't have heard it earlier, when I was supposed to, and maybe I didn't try hard enough and why did I give up and how much more could he have given me and why wasn't I grateful and, and and and . . .

"I want to be who he wants me to be," I say. It's so simple and should be so doable, because he's been training me to be exactly that person for my whole entire life. "I want to be Little Luck."

"But you're you instead," Zelda says. It comes out of her mouth easy, and it's weird how simple it sounds because it feels completely impossible.

I listen again for the sound of magic. I could use it right now, the promise of something big and special and lucky come to save me.

But then I look at Lyle. And Zelda. And the uncle I never knew I had.

And maybe they are that big and special and lucky thing that is saving me.

And maybe I am too.

Forty-six

"So it's going back to the lake, like Lyle said, right?" I say. "It might be sort of hard. It will probably take a while."

Uncle Bennett nods. "Most good things take a while," he says. "Most good things are a little hard, too."

It's the opposite of what my father told me. He promised that good things, like magic, would come easily, would find me naturally.

But I am learning there's a lot my father wasn't right about.

"So we're just gonna just drop the jars into the lake?" Zelda asks. I shake my head.

"No, they'd be found in two minutes. Dad would come right back here and gather them all up."

"Well then, what are we supposed to do?" Zelda looks at the lake. It's cold out, and the lake looks even colder.

"Open them underwater. Say . . . something. And I guess hope for the best," I say.

"Say something," Lyle says. I think maybe he's mad at me, but he's smiling. "Rose Alice Anders, Little Luck, has a great plan, and it's to say *something*." He shakes his head and laughs.

"Say 'no more magic,'" I say. "Okay?"

"Really?"

"Seems like a safe thing to say. I don't know. It's what we want. And if magic can make things happen, maybe it can . . . make things not happen."

Lyle closes his eyes. I wonder if he's thinking about all the books he's read on the topic, all the many, many pages of secret learning about magic that happened alone in his room.

"No more magic," he says, trying it out. "It's very simple."

"I think it might work," Uncle Bennett says. "It's sort of—well, it's sort of what I did. I wished for no more magic, and the magic stayed away. It's what you did too, didn't you, Rose? During your capturing?" He says it like it's an obvious thing.

"No," I say. "All I ever wanted was magic. It didn't want me." They're Dad's words, though, and I let myself wonder if maybe they aren't quite true. Sometimes—sort of often—I wondered why Dad had all that magic and why anyone needed one hundred sixty-one jars of anything, and most of all I wondered what the point of all those jars was, if they'd never been able to fix the thing that most needed fixing—my family.

"You're sure you didn't tell the magic to stay away?" Uncle Bennett says. He tilts his head. I wonder what I look like to him. If I remind him of his daughters or of my dad or of their dad or of someone else from their family who I know nothing about.

"Maybe I didn't quite believe magic was the most important thing in the world," I say, which is about one-tenth of the whole answer, but it's the part I can say right now.

"If you tell it to stay away, it will," Uncle Bennett says. "Magic is there because we want it to be. I think releasing it into the lake—"

"Let's do it," Lyle says, which is what I needed him to say. I need us to be on the same page, to have the same plan, to be in it together. Because Wendell Anders has been wrong about a lot of things, but one of the biggest ones is staying away from his brother. So I pull mine close and hand Lyle a jar. It's pink and fluffy inside. I take one too. It glows a radioactive blue brightness.

We run into the lake. I think he's going to hit the water first—his legs are longer and faster than mine—but he slows down right as his toes touch the first wave, and we dive in together, push ourselves below the surface of the water, take the tops off our jars, and say, through the lake water, "No more magic." Maybe I can't hear him and maybe he can't hear me, but maybe, maybe, the magic can hear us both.

It takes hours, releasing it all, even with the help of Uncle Bennett and Zelda. Even when we run fast and say the words fast and get good at opening the jars in one quick movement. It's still a long, exhausting process, the lake filling with all kinds of magic, the water turning shades of pink and red and green, a whooshing noise getting louder and louder.

"What is all that magic going to do?" Zelda asks after an especially full jar of spiky, silvery magic gets released. But we don't know, so we can't answer. I can hear the magic now and see it making the waves bigger. I can feel it too, a sort of wind running through my bones, a tremble and shake and excitement for what comes next. A worry, too.

We keep going. We're in it, and releasing the magic feels like releasing so many things. I always thought—Dad always told us—that having as many jars as possible made us safe and better. That life was more beautiful with every bit of captured magic. But as the magic slides away into the water, I feel lighter and lighter, less and less worried, less scared, more alive. I feel more like myself, if I even know who myself is, which I don't really, but without all that magic hanging around, maybe I can find out.

After a hundred jars, the rain starts.

And after two hundred, it's the wind.

When we are on the last few jars, the lake lurches and rolls. Usually a storm comes from the sky, pouring down. But this storm moves upward from the lake.

It's a multicolored storm. A storm of lake water and magic and something else, too, something even more powerful than magic pulsing through the air, making it beautiful and loud.

I never got to make my rainbow. I never got to do the things with magic that I imagined. But I made this storm, and it is bigger and better than anything else I could have done, because I know it is all the magic I will ever do. It is better than pink hair and parties and learning violin and making Evan Dell be my boyfriend.

It is saying goodbye to something that hurt, seeing it light up the lake and the shore and the sky and Zelda's eyes and Lyle's, too, and knowing we chose to let it go, we chose this moment right here.

I don't want magic anymore, but I know what it is to have a big force in your life and want something for yourself. A little bit of something that you can control or fix or make your own. Maybe that's what the magic was for Dad. Him trying, so, so hard, to finally get to choose how things would be, to make the world the way he wanted it to look when he was small with a father who scared him and a family that didn't quite protect him and a world that felt wrong more often than it felt right.

Maybe he just wanted things to feel right.

And somehow, magic made it all wrong.

Forty-seven

"What have you done?" His voice is a boom, thundering louder than the storm.

Here he is, at TooBlue Lake, as if the storm called him here. It's still raging, and must be in Belling Bright, too, because Dad's soaked to the bone and shivering and looks, for the first time ever, scared.

I can tell from how my uncle Bennett looks at him that it's not the first time *he's* seen my father scared. Not by a long shot.

"Bennett," Dad says. He looks at his brother, and something passes between them. A whole bunch of somethings, a whole lifetime of talking and then not talking, of being in the same room at night and telling all their secrets and of being in the same town for years but never speaking. And maybe it's nice for a moment, maybe it's the way Lyle and I sometimes look at each other over the dinner table—*Did you see that? Are you here with me? Are we in this together? Will we take care of each other? Yes and yes and yes and yes.*

But then the nice thing turns not nice and Dad's jaw tightens and his arms cross over his chest and he takes a breath and holds it, like by holding that breath in he's holding a lot of stuff in, and we all know what that stuff is, even if we don't want to say it out loud.

"We're going home," Dad says, and it's quiet, but the bad kind of quiet.

"Wendell," our uncle Bennett says. "It's for the best."

"What is?" Dad asks.

"You're not meant for it either, you know. I've always thought that." Zelda's dad says it so calmly even though it's the worst thing he could ever say to my father.

"You think *I'm* Not Meant for Magic?" Dad asks. His voice explodes now, back to itself, and a laugh spills out too, but it's a sharp laugh, one that isn't meant to include anyone else in it.

"Look what it's done to you," Uncle Bennett says.

"Given me and my family everything we've ever wanted? Given us respect and acclaim? Made everything beautiful? Made everyone happy?" Dad's shouting now. He's getting closer to Uncle Bennett, and I'm watching his fingers and his arms, keeping track of the ways his muscles twitch and tighten and strain, wondering where all that energy and noise will *go*.

I think about those long evenings in our front yard. How cold my toes were without shoes. How impossible catching fireflies felt. How my lungs would burn from all the running and jumping and trying. How bad I'd feel for Lyle, ignored and alone inside, and then how bad I'd feel for me, for not getting to ever be ignored and alone and inside. I think about reporters and Ginger and Maddy and how feeling like I was better than them seemed fun but actually only made me feel like I wasn't one of them, and how I'm not one of them, not one of anyone, really, and how that feels awkward and wrong but also more right than it felt trying to be Little Luck and failing.

"I wasn't ever really that happy," I say, and maybe I shouldn't have said it, but it's so true it makes my mouth dry, so I have to.

"Of course you were," Dad says. He looks almost sad, like all this time all he's wanted was to make me happy and he's seeing that he failed.

"Were you?" I ask. "When you were little?"

Dad shakes his head like the question doesn't matter, but I know that it does. "You had it so much better than me," he says. And I know he thinks that is true. But for the

306

first time in my whole life, what my dad thinks is true isn't the same as the truth.

I move my wrist in circles. All this rain is making it ache, like always. Dad turns away from me.

"You took my magic away from me," Dad whispers to Uncle Bennett.

"It's different than when Dad took your magic away from you," Uncle Bennett says. "He did that to be cruel. We did this to save you. To save your kids. To start to right all the things that are wrong."

"He never wanted me to have anything good, and neither do you," Dad says. "All those years, I protected you from him. He'd get mad and I'd step right in. And he'd take every jar of my magic for himself, wasting it all. I got punished for protecting you, and here you are, doing it to me again. You never appreciated—"

"Of course I appreciated—" Uncle Bennett starts.

"*This* is appreciation? This? This is what you do?"

"You thought the solution was more magic. I thought the solution was less." My uncle tries to put an arm around my father. There's so much about my father's childhood that I'll never know. But I see that my father had been brave and that he had also been angry and sad and kind and mean and jealous and alone.

I know about all of those things. I know how you can be

all of them at once. I want him to lean against Uncle Bennett now, and be the kind and good part of himself.

But instead Dad's hands fly into the air and he propels himself toward my uncle, who isn't meant for magic, and isn't meant for this either, for my father's rages, for my father's anger. My uncle wasn't meant for any of this, shouldn't have been involved, shouldn't have helped us, should have been allowed to stay in his home with his family forgetting all about us.

It's my fault.

I'm the one who deserves it. So I leap in between my uncle and my father and let my body take the impact, which is powerful, which hurts, which is my father's hands shoving me, hard, so hard I fall onto the ground, so hard I lose my breath, so hard the evidence of this exact moment right now will be visible on my shoulder blades and where Dad's elbow hit my chin and in the bones of my wrist, which crack when they hit the ground, trying to catch me, trying to keep me upright, but fumbling and giving in under the weight of me and him and this.

Forty-eight

The doctor looks sad as he holds the x-rays up to the light. Dad wanted to take me alone, but no one would let him. Uncle Bennett, Lyle, and Zelda are all huddled in the room with us. Mom is on her way. Dad keeps saying she didn't want to get involved with all the worrying about jars of magic and who took them where, that she doesn't understand what's at stake, that she doesn't really understand magic like the rest of us.

But I think Mom understands magic pretty well. I remember her disappointed look when Dad did the UnTired magic, the way she was always wary of using it for anything that mattered. How she'd sprinkle it onto burnt cookies and make them un-burnt and say that's about all magic is good for. We always thought that meant she was silly and small.

I don't know why we never listened to her. I guess the reason is simple, though. Because that's what Dad told us.

I want her here now. I want her non-magically-minded self looking at my wrist and asking the doctor questions and smoothing out my hair and telling me it's okay to cry.

"You keep hurting this wrist, huh?" the doctor says to me in a small voice. He doesn't look at my father. My father doesn't look at me.

"What do you mean?" I ask.

"This wrist," the doctor says. "I can see on the x-ray that—"

"She's fine," Dad interrupts. "She's never hurt anything. She's a healthy Anders girl."

"Wendell," Uncle Bennett says. He stands up. He is the same height as my father, but I see him trying to pull himself up higher, taller, bigger in this moment.

"Look at her. She's fine. You ever hurt your wrist before, Rose?" Dad asks. His voice is gruff and he's talking too fast, and I can see his jaw clench.

I roll my wrist around in a circle again. Like I always do when it gives me a phantom pain, except this time the pain is urgent and strong and I know where it came from. That other ghostly pain has always been strange and unexplained and brushed off.

But *there*. It has always been *there*.

"I don't remember anything happening, but it hurts when it rains. And other times. It sort of aches, sometimes."

"That happens after a break," the doctor says.

"But I never broke it," I say.

The doctor points to a place on the x-ray. It's not something I'd ever notice. It's a tiny strip of blank space where bone should be, a nothing of a mark, except it's everything. It's an answer. "Right here," he says. "Didn't heal great the last time it broke."

Dad shakes his head and paces the room.

Uncle Bennett leans in to get a better look at the mark. And Lyle hangs his head.

Zelda's the only one who will really look at me. And she does. She looks at me and asks with her eyes if I'm okay, and I answer with my eyes and a quiver of my chin that I am not, and she slides next to me. "We're here," she says. "We know."

I don't know Zelda very well. It will take a long time for me to know her the way I know Ginger. But I trust her anyway. Maybe because of her flower crown or the way her eyes never dart away when she speaks. Maybe because she's my cousin. Or maybe because she's Not Meant for Magic and neither am I and neither is anyone else, but she understood that before the rest of us.

The doctor doesn't say any more about the wrist to me, but he asks my father to stay, and when my mother arrives—teary and hugging me so tight I almost can't breathe—he tells her to stay, too.

He wraps my wrist gently and hums a tune I can't quite catch while he does it.

Uncle Bennett doesn't leave my side. He doesn't touch me, but he makes sure I know he is there. He's like a tall tree, steady and there if you ever need something to lean against.

"Do you ever use magic to do this?" I ask the doctor. He has to do so much squinting and inspecting and snipping, I assume it would be easier to do with a jar of magic. And I can see jars lined up on his desk, ready to be used.

"Never," he says.

"Wouldn't it be easier?"

"I'm sure it would."

"So why don't you?" I ask. Dad's shifting in the corner of the room. He's used magic a hundred times when we could have gone to the doctor instead. We go for checkups, but never if we're sick or hurting. Not until today, and today we're only here because Uncle Bennett insisted.

"I'll tell you a secret," the doctor says. "Magic can only fix the surface of things. Magic can change what you see, but it can't change anything deep down. And you never know how long it will last. We're more powerful than magic. That's the truth."

My dad clears his throat. Zelda begins to smile. I wonder

why Dad never told me that. For all the years he spent telling me what magic is and why it matters and what to do with it, he never mentioned that maybe I could do even more without it.

He told me I was lucky thousands of times.

But he never once told me I was powerful all on my own.

Forty-nine

"*Again?*" *Ginger says* at school two days later.

Our desks are still next to each other, so Ginger is close enough to touch my cast, which she does, quickly, and then retreats.

"What do you mean, 'again'?" I ask. People are watching us, but I don't care anymore.

"Oh," Ginger says. She blushes like she doesn't want to say, so she says it to her desk instead of me. "There was that time your broke your—your wrist got broken before. And your dad fixed it with magic."

"You remember that?" I ask.

"You don't?" Ginger replies. She looks a little sad, like it's a memory I need, and I try to find it. If I used my one jar of magic, maybe it would be for this—remembering whatever it is that Ginger remembers. But I don't want to use magic, and I don't have to. Ginger is here. And maybe we aren't exactly what we were before, but I don't need that. I need to know the things she knows about the way things used to be.

"When was it?" I ask. I think about that nothing-mark on my x-ray, how sure the doctor was that I'd broken my wrist before, and what he said, about magic not really fixing anything below the surface.

"Years ago," Ginger says. "Maybe four years ago? We were, I don't know, seven or eight. You were tiny. You were into wearing a lot of purple."

"I still wear purple," I say.

"I know, but like a *lot*," Ginger says, and we both laugh a little because it's almost sort of an inside joke, and maybe my friendship with Ginger will be okay and we'll have things we used to have—inside jokes and knowing things about each other that other people don't, and whispering in a room full of people who are trying to listen.

Maybe.

Or maybe we'll have something else entirely.

"What happened?" I ask.

"I don't know exactly," Ginger says.

"You can tell me," I say.

"I can't, I really don't know. We were playing. We

knocked over some jars of magic. Your dad came in—"

"Knocked over?" I ask. The memory is on the edge of my brain, but it isn't quite mine yet. It sounds familiar, like a story someone told me once but not in a great long while.

"By accident. We were playing and crashed into a table with jars on it. We lost some magic. It flew out. Nothing much happened. Some ivy grew on the ceiling. Lyle couldn't stop laughing for like two hours because of some sort of laughter magic. It was green and sparkly and jumpy. It was small magic. But your dad was mad."

"How mad?" I ask, but I know.

"Mad, Rose," Ginger says. "I hid my eyes. And I opened them again when I heard a snap and you were on the floor and your dad was above you and breathing sort of heavy and you were crying, but Lyle was still laughing from the magic and your dad went and got that cloud magic really fast and it fixed everything. Or not everything, I guess, but it fixed your wrist. He said not to worry about it and not to worry your mom with it because she would only get upset about it."

"Cloud magic?" I ask. I wonder how many things Ginger remembers that I don't. Then I wonder how many things I remember that Ginger doesn't. And how many things we both do, but in wildly different ways. That friendship can exist somehow, in all those different rememberings, is kind of amazing, when I think about it. I lean closer to Ginger. Maybe someday we'll remember this time, when we were twelve and everything changed, and we'll have to tell each other different parts of the story, and the truth will be somewhere in the middle of all the different ways we remember it.

"It was this tiny jar," Ginger says. "We loved it, remember? A tiny jar with the world's smallest, fluffiest cloud inside. Like, a perfect cloud. Not a rainy stormy cloud. A floaty one. But smaller than your fingernail. In that little jar. We'd always ask your dad what kind of magic it was."

It's the cloud I remember, at last. The way it floated in the jar. The perfect symmetry of it.

When Dad opened the jar, he held it right up to my wrist. The cloud felt exactly like I thought it would—soft and transparent, a whisper of a feeling. And like that, my wrist was fine. There was the pain—I am now remembering the pain, but only because it's the same pain that I felt at TooBlue Lake—and then the sudden vanishing of it.

Magic.

"We didn't have any magic this time," I say, lifting my arm a little to remind her of the cast on it. Not that she'd forgotten.

"Your dad has more magic than anyone," Ginger says.

"Not anymore," I say, and I tell her what we did.

And I tell her what I've been thinking. What the doctor said. The thought that won't leave my brain or heart alone.

317

"I want everyone to put their magic in the lake," I say. "I don't think anyone should have any. I don't think I believe in it. And maybe I never did."

A few weeks ago, maybe Ginger would have told everyone in class what I've said and made sure they all knew how weird and wrong I am. And maybe if Maddy heard me now, that's what she'd do. But Ginger just keeps looking at my wrist. She's thinking. And remembering, I guess. And maybe she's really hearing me.

Fifty

A Story I Had Forgotten
About Ginger and Her Family That Is Also About
Me and My Family

When Ginger's dad was sick, my dad offered to help with all these jars of magic. Ten of them, maybe. I helped carry them.

"We're going to fix him," I told Ginger. She was quiet. She was quiet all the time when he was sick, and it made me louder, because I wanted to fill up all the space her being quiet left. I wanted her to feel like nothing was changing, so I talked and talked and talked. "My dad can fix anything," I said. And Ginger was still quiet.

Dad went upstairs to see Ginger's father. He was up there awhile. Once, the house shook. Once, we heard what sounded like a symphony playing something really beautiful. Once the sky turned orange for a bit, then it turned back to blue.

I kept talking to Ginger. About a TV show I was watching and about Lyle's annoying singing voice and about what I wanted to do over summer break. And about magic. Ginger nodded sometimes, but she didn't say a word. We put on a movie she loved and she curled into the couch like it might swallow her up, and the day turned to night, and when Dad came downstairs his face was drawn and he looked tired and his jars were empty.

"Is he okay?" Ginger said, her first words all day, and maybe they were the only words her brain could think or her mouth could form those days.

"I think we did it," Dad said. "Magic knows the way. Magic knows what's best. Magic will do what it's supposed to do." He kept nodding and I gave him this huge hug because he was saving Ginger's dad and that meant he was saving Ginger, too, and I was so, so proud that he was my father and so, so hopeful that I would be as magical as him, someday.

Ginger looked worried. She ran upstairs. Her mother mumbled a thank you, but it wasn't a very big one, and Dad and I sort of snuck out without anyone really saying goodbye.

Halfway home, Dad sighed. "They don't understand," he said. "They don't listen, that family. They don't take magic seriously. That's the problem. Magic is serious. It's everything."

I didn't know what he meant, but I didn't really want to ask, either. Sometimes, asking only made things worse. So when I could help it, I tried not to ask too much.

But it sounded, a little bit, like Dad thought it was Ginger's family's fault that her dad was sick. And it sounded, sort of, like magic wasn't going to fix him after all.

Ginger's dad was gone within a day.

"I tried," my father said on our way to the funeral.

"Of course you did," Mom said, next to him in the front seat, wiping away tears by the second.

"If there was just more magic—" Dad said.

"Let's not talk about magic today," Mom said. The tears were coming faster. She was having trouble keeping up with them. "Not everything's about magic. I'm getting sick and tired of magic, frankly."

Dad stopped the car. "Fine," he said. "You get yourself there, then."

Lyle and I froze in the backseat. When Dad got mad, it usually took more time than that. There was usually a path from normal to not-normal that we could trace and know how to fix and do better next time.

"Wendell," Mom said. "Please. This isn't about you."

"Get out of the car," Dad said. His voice was the bad kind of calm.

"It's important we're all there," Mom said.

"I said get out," Dad said. "I won't say it again."

And so we did. Because once Dad has decided something, his mind doesn't change.

Mom got out first and Lyle and I followed and Mom was quiet, just like Ginger had been.

This time, though, I didn't try to fill up all that silent space with anything. I was pretty sure there was nothing that would work, anyway.

Not even magic.

Especially not magic.

Fifty-one

At the end of the school day, Ginger finds me.

"Let's go," she says.

"Go where?" I ask. Maybe a few months ago, when we were still best friends, I wouldn't have had to ask what she meant. I would have just *known*. But I don't know this Ginger in front of me, with her pink hair and perfect clothes and twenty jars of magic.

"To the lake," she says. "I told my mom. She says she'll drive us. So all that's left is you saying you'll go with us."

"TooBlue Lake?" I ask, as if there's some other lake we might go to.

"Obviously. I'm ready. I want to get rid of my magic

too." She beams. Her fingers tremble a little, like the excitement has to shiver out of her body.

"But you love magic," I say.

"What makes you think that?" Ginger looks actually confused, which makes no sense, because all she's done since New Year's is make magic happen. And make fun of me for not having any magic. And choose to only be friends with people who *do* have magic.

"I mean—everything that's happened makes me think that," I say.

"Well, everything that's happened would have made me think *you* love magic, too," she says. She raises her eyebrows. I can't argue with her. Not after a lifetime of being Little Luck. "But I guess maybe you never had a chance to think something different."

"I guess."

"I've had time to think too," she says. "And every time I think magic is going to fix stuff it's just made things worse."

I could ask her what she means. But she grabs her dad's ring around her neck and she looks extra long at me, and I don't have to ask, because I already know. We've been waiting our whole lives to be twelve, so that we could finally have magic and finally make everything be the way we wanted it to be.

But her dad's still gone and our friendship got ruined

and I have a broken wrist and nothing really got fixed or better or even all that magical.

So maybe it's not even such a big deal, to release it all into a lake. Because maybe it was never really what we wanted it to be.

Ginger doesn't wait for me to wade in with her. She swims out far into the lake and bobs up and down in the water, opening jar after jar after jar.

When she swims back to me, she's shivering but smiling.

"Who else should we get to come here?" she asks with the world's biggest grin.

And maybe there's no one else who wants to give up their magic. But maybe, maybe, if Ginger and I both see how it was never really what it promised to be, maybe there are more of us.

There's a gust of wind and a tiny rain shower from Ginger's unloading of magic into the lake. And we stand in the drizzle for a while, because we can. Because it feels good to be here. Because we don't have anywhere else we have to be.

Fifty-two

It *doesn't happen* all at once. It doesn't happen with the whole town, or even with busloads of kids. It happens as slowly and lightly as that drizzle from the day Ginger let go of her magic. It happens when people ask us why we did it, and when we introduce them to Zelda and Bennett and Lucy and Elizabeth. It happens when we don't expect it, from people we don't expect.

It happens when we're there and also when we are not.

It happens. People let go of their magic. Some people. Not many. But enough so that when we gather on Zelda's front lawn to make flower crowns and talk about what we'll do on New Year's Day, when everyone else is at the lake, the lawn is crowded and I have to squeeze to sit in between Zelda and Ginger. I wave at Lyle across the lawn with some of his friends and I can't believe this was a place I never knew existed until just a few months ago.

I try to understand what we look like, the Not Meant for Magic. I try to see something we all have in common, a way we hold our hands or how our flower crowns look. But I can't see anything in particular. Just, I guess, that we mostly look happy, or at least we look like we're here, like we're not thinking of other things we could be doing, other people we could turn out to be.

Zelda's flower crown is the most complicated. It's braided and has different sizes of dandelions and wraps around her head not once or even twice but five whole times, something I had said was impossible without magic. But she said she could do cool things without magic, and she was right.

My dandelion crown isn't very good. I haven't learned the art of it, even though I have been living here with Zelda and her family—which is my family—for a month. I don't like all the sitting still and all the not-talking and all the very careful work of making small knots and lining things up. So I make sloppy dandelion crowns where you can see all the knots. You can see the work of it, how hard I had to try, how it didn't come easily to me, how it wasn't simple and pretty and nice.

I am not simple and pretty and nice.

And I am not lucky.

A woman in brown shoes with a tight smile taps me on the shoulder. "You're an inspiration," she says. I recognize her. The shoes and the smile and also the voice, which is smaller now than when I first heard it, less sure of where it's going, too. But sweeter.

The reporter. I look for her notebook, her leather bag, her tape recorder. But she's in jeans and her hair is a little messy and her hands are tucked into her back pockets.

"I'm sorry," I say. "I don't want to talk to reporters."

"Oh, I'm not here for that," she says. "I'm here because I—I did it too. Went to the lake. Opened the jars. Said goodbye to all that."

I take her in again. It's not just that she's wearing jeans and smiling. It's that she looks comfortable in those jeans and the smile is new, is not trying to be something else.

"Oh," I say. "Well. Welcome, then, I guess."

"You're a hero," she says. "I just want you to know that. You're Little Luck after all, you know?"

"Oh," I say again. "No. I'm not. I don't want to be. I'm just Rose. I just did what I needed to do. And other people did what they needed to do. And here we are."

"It's not that simple," she says. "You shouldn't be so humble. You're the reason we're all here."

I shake my head. Hard. I don't want to be that person. I don't want to be Little Luck or a hero or the reason for anything. I don't want to be known. Not like that, not anymore. She might not be writing an article about me, but she's writing my story anyway, trying to make it something other than what it is to me.

"I guess—aren't *you* the reason you're here?" I try to see what brought her here, what it was that made her stop believing in magic.

She smiles. It's a big smile, a real one. And it doesn't matter why she's here, it just matters that she is, and that all these people are. We're all here. I give the reporter a handful of dandelions. "It's fun," I say with a shrug. Sometimes in Belling Bright we wanted things to be more than what they were. Dandelions that turned glittery or grew three sizes, crowns that made you invisible, made you beautiful, made you able to run faster than anyone else in town.

We don't need things to be more than what they are anymore. The reporter sits down and starts knotting the stems. I wonder what hers will look like, when she's done.

"How's my crown?" Ginger asks. She braids her crown lying on her back, which looks impossible but I guess isn't. She braids it with one eye open and one eye closed, to get the best view of it, and her fingers are quick with it, like Zelda's, not slow like mine.

We are settling back into friendship. Except it isn't the same friendship as before. It's new and different and sometimes it feels sort of awkward, like we are a messy, badly knotted dandelion crown, and I guess we really sort of *are*. We are people who can't quite find the right way to tie ourselves to each other but are trying anyway.

Which is good, because I need Ginger now, more than ever. My father is getting help somewhere far away from Belling Bright and my mother is trying to understand why she stayed when things were so bad, and my world feels disjointed and strange. Ginger is someone safe in all of that newness.

But her crown makes me feel jealous, a quick familiar feeling of all the things she has and all the things I don't, but instead of getting lost in it, I start another flower crown and decide to make the messy knots bigger, the sloppiness sloppier, the design of it floppier and less lined up and less perfect.

And it starts to look beautiful too. Not beautiful like Zelda's or Ginger's. But the work of it is right there on the surface, and when I put it on it falls over one eye a little and I like that mistake, too.

"Yours is great," I say to Ginger.

"So is yours," she says.

We pass the afternoon like this, Zelda, Ginger, and I

and a few dozen other people who want things to be different, who let go of jars of magic for another kind of magic, the kind that's just the magic of the sun on the top of your head and a free day stretching out ahead.

Eventually I get my sketch pad and I draw people on Zelda's lawn. An old man in flannel, a group of teenage girls covered in dandelions, laughing about something. Two men leaning against each other and their two kids climbing all over them. Then I draw myself and my dandelion crown and the sunset that isn't magical at all—just gray streaks against a blueish sky, nothing particularly beautiful, but I like trying to capture the exact shape of the clouds, the exact shadows of the disappearing sun on all of our faces.

Somewhere, Evan Dell is opening a jar of magic to make himself better at baseball. Somewhere Maddy and Layla are magicking their legs longer, their hair shinier, their houses bigger. Somewhere, my father is unwinding his past and his present and maybe, maybe, deciding on a different kind of future.

And if he does, maybe we'll find a way to be in it with him. Without magic. Without a lot of things that never should have been.

Somewhere my mother is looking at houses in the center of town, where parents move when they split up. She promised me we'd keep coats in the coat closets and not on the couches, and that we could each keep our one jar of magic wherever we wanted.

I wonder, now, where I'll keep it. What kind of house we'll be in. When we'll see my father next, and what it will feel like if we do.

My one jar of magic will probably go in my closet at my new house. Somewhere behind my fancy holidays outfits and the bin with old report cards and school photos. It will be a thing that I have, not a thing that I am.

I don't know who I am yet. I am Rose Alice Anders. I have a crooked dandelion crown on my head and two best friends and a brother who is maybe a third best friend and an uncle who speaks slowly and quietly and makes a much prettier dandelion crown than I can make.

I am not the most magical person in all of Belling Bright. Not even close.

I'm not the best at dandelion crowns either. Or sitting still. Or telling stories. Or finding a boyfriend or girlfriend. Or playing soccer. Or being not-jealous of things that no one really needs to be jealous of.

But maybe I am the best at something. Maybe I am the best at drawing this sunset exactly as it is, the best at making a sloppy crown, the best at stitching myself back together after something that changed everything, the best at changing a little bit with it, the best at finding family where I didn't know there would be any, the best at hiding one jar of magic in the closet and letting that tiny dot of wonder be enough.

Because I am Rose Alice Anders, and I am not Little Luck, but I am one tiny dot of wonder too. And it is enough.

Author's Note

Our homes, our families, should always be safe places for everyone—adults and children alike. But this is not always the case. If you don't feel safe at home, or if you are concerned about a friend's safety, you deserve to be heard and protected and believed. It is important to understand that in most cases, authorities are required to get involved if children aren't safe in their homes or with their families. If you are ready to take that step, you should reach out to a trusted adult for help. Trusted adults can be family, friends, teachers, counselors, doctors, or anyone who has shown you that they are good listeners and respect you and your feelings.

If you don't feel safe at home, it isn't your fault. You

deserve to be safe, no matter what.

If you would like to know more about domestic violence, or need further resources, there are some organizations that can help you. Here are a few:

The Childhelp National Child Abuse Hotline
1-800-422-4453
childhelp.org
This organization can help with both prevention and intervention, and their hotline is a place to turn if you need support, information, or action.

Prevent Child Abuse America
preventchildabuse.org
This organization both promotes and develops programs and services that work to eradicate domestic violence. They are invested in evidence-based programs that address the needs of families in distress, including the home-visiting program Healthy Families America.

The National Domestic Violence Hotline
1-800-799-7233
thehotline.org
At this organization, trained professionals are on hand 24/7 to take calls related to domestic violence. They

can offer tools and support for a person experiencing
domestic violence, or a person concerned about a
friend's domestic situation.

You are always worthy of a safe home.
There are people who can help.
You are not alone.

Acknowledgments

There are always so many people to thank, because it takes so very many people to usher an idea into a story and a story into a book. It is magic, truly, every step of it.

Thank you to my agent, Victoria Marini, for being you, being in my corner, and for all the work you've done over the years. I would like to capture your energy and passion in a jar.

Thank you to my editor, Mabel Hsu, for bringing so much heart and humor and depth to our work together. You gave me confidence and excitement and such a stronger, greater understanding of what this story was meant to be. I would like to capture your magical mind in a jar.

Thank you to Katherine Tegen for giving me a publishing home and so much support. And I couldn't be more grateful for everyone at Katherine Tegen Books and HarperCollins who bring their creativity, spirit, precision, and love to every book you work on—Tanu Srivastava, Sam Benson, Bethany Reis, Alexandra Rakaczki, Emma Meyer, Kimberly Stella—I am profoundly inspired by your work and dedication. Thank you to incredible cover designer, Laura Mock, and illustrator, Jane Newland, who made this book look so dreamy and special.

Thank you to the magical Vermont College of Fine Arts. Though I am a faculty member, I learn so much in my time there, and this book changed and grew and blossomed because of time spent in Vermont and the lessons learned from students and faculty alike.

And thank you as always to friends and family who support me in hundreds of big and small ways. Little sparks of the love you give me show up on every page.

And thank you to Frank and Fia, for all the magic, all the time.